Also from this publisher

Mexican Kaleidoscope: myths, mysteries and mystique
Western Mexico, a Traveler's Treasury
Lake Chapala Through the Ages, an anthology of travelers' tales
Mexico by Motorcycle: An Adventure Story and Guide
Geo-Mexico, the geography and dynamics of modern Mexico

DILEMMA

DILEMMA

JAN DUNLAP

SB
SOMBRERO BOOKS, B.C., CANADA

ISBN 978-0-9952889-6-6
First edition 2017
Text © 2017 by Jan Dunlap
This edition © 2017 by Sombrero Books
Cover artwork: Oliver Rivas

Sombrero Books, Box 4, Ladysmith B.C. V9G 1A1, Canada

This book is in memory of my best friend, Eva Tyrrel, my walking partner, mentor and collaborator who urged me to put some of my mental meanderings on paper. She passed, of cancer, at far too young an age.

Rest in peace.

Te amo,

Jan.

INTRODUCTION

Natalie was thinking of her last assignment—art forgeries in Europe—and wishing she could spend more time with her significant other. Alas, she is on her way to Mexico to try and find out what she can about the stories of government involvement in the drug dealing in the small town to which she has been assigned. Thinking it would be "déjà vu", she had no inkling of the dilemma she was about to face.

1

NATALIE

Pearl Buck wrote, "Inside myself is a place where I live alone, and that's where you renew your springs that never dry up." It was the second day of my vacation and I had not left my large old drafty apartment. My springs needed a lot of renewing. My last assignment, in Greece, had nearly bought me a grave marker. The agency was singing my praises for a job well done while apologizing for nearly getting me killed. Andrew Martin, my supervisor, had smiled at me as I left the office two days ago and said, "Natalie, it really would have been a waste."

The gleam in his gray-green eyes, and my reflection looking back at me in the lobby mirror, whispered in my ear that he did not refer to my job performance. My looks have proven to be both an asset and a liability in my chosen field. I've been a DEA agent for six years. I'm thirty years old. My natural red hair, large green eyes, and small waist are, I have been told, memorable. On the other hand, I have found it easy to get accepted into almost any group, in any country, because of my looks.

Looking out over the ocean, listening to Neil Diamond sing love songs, I hardly heard my phone ring. The mood interrupted, I lowered the volume on my stereo and picked up the phone. Some people never learn.

Andrew's "hello" should have made me hang it up before he had time to speak further.

"Just a minute, please listen. Read page two, second column, of today's *LA Times*, catch a plane and come into the office at 9.00am tomorrow, just to talk," he said and quickly hung up the phone.

It was the "please" that got me searching through the stack of newspapers by the back door. He never said please. "U.S. seeks to extradite eight people from Mexico," read the bold black heading, halfway down the page. According to its source, the eight people on its list were all drug trafficking from Mexico into the United States. One of the people on the list was Enrique Vázquez, a known trafficker on the Federal Bureau of Investigation's "Ten Most Wanted" list.

I talked with myself for the rest of an otherwise peaceful afternoon and evening. "Those dirty, rotten, despicable bastards," I said every few minutes, not referring to the drug traffickers. "It won't work!" I yelled. "Screw you!" I cried.

The next morning at 9.45am I walked into the office. The bastards had to wait for forty five minutes, hopefully wondering if I was going to show. Fuck Andrew, he knew I would.

I had read about the little village of Ajijic, in the state of Jalisco, and the unique foreign colony of expatriates who lived there, but never thought I would be going there involved in a covert drug operation. More and more I was beginning to see the drug situation was out of control. My last assignment had made me realize how involved it was, and on what a massive scale: people known on a national and international level. Exciting times but dangerous for a woman alone. I wanted out and often thought of trying to leave the agency but it was like having a tiger by the tail.

As the plane soared over Mexico, I tried to put my dark thoughts on the back burner. Closing my eyes, I told myself that someone had to do it and I was the perfect candidate for a drug agent. A loner all of my life, I was an only child of an alcoholic, social climbing mother and a brilliant history professor, who spent his life steeped in books on ancient civilization. My only confidant was Clarissa, my parent's cook. Since I was five years old Clarissa had been protecting me from my mother's alcoholic moods. She had seen me through all of my trials as a child and teenager. She was still the person I went back home to see.

My thoughts wouldn't be still. Where would it lead? I wondered. The four day briefing in Washington had been long and explicit. There was no doubt that gigantic amounts of drugs were being moved through Mexico. The California and Texas borders were standing invitations to drug dealers, on both large and small scales.

My supervisor, Andrew Martin, was beginning to suspect one of his top agents in Mexico of double dealing. This was to be part of my assignment, to find out if it was true.

He turned Hoffman's dossier over to me. Meanwhile he told me how Hoffman had worked his way into the biggest drug operation they had uncovered to date. According to him, it had taken Hoffman about two years of small time smuggling and name dropping to get where he was within the organization. He suspected Hoffman had been corrupted along the way by the high rolling, high living people whom he had met. He believed Hoffman still had some loyalty to the DEA, and maybe could be brought back into the fold.

It sure wouldn't be the first time someone had "gone astray." The DEA was riddled with stories to that effect. It was almost like having a key to your own bank.

Andrew knew Hoffman liked women, and was always looking. Hoffman had bragged about partying with his boss, Enrique Vázquez. Vázquez was head of the organization and highly respected for his education and ability to pull such a lucrative operation together.

Andrew was hoping I would be able to bring both of them to heel. He had a lot more faith in my abilities than I had. My last assignment in Greece had left me pretty shaken up. I had spent some harrowing, dangerous moments while there, but had come out victorious. Hoffman had implied to Andrew that there were some pretty high level politicians involved with this drug lord, but he had been hesitant to mention names and this made Andrew suspicious.

It appeared to me that sometimes in Washington the left hand doesn't know about the right one. What was most frightening to me was if high level politicians were involved, did any of them have access to my dossier? How well was I hidden? Since the powers that be already suspected my contact in Mexico of working both sides, I knew I would have to watch my back constantly. "It's best to get on with it and not think of what's ahead," I thought.

The voice of our pilot broke into my meditation assuring the passengers the climate in Guadalajara would be divine, just a slight breeze, seventy two degrees. Looking below through the window, the mountains looked as if they were covered in velvet carpeting.

As the plane came over the mountains, I got my first view of Lake Chapala, Mexico's largest lake. It was breathtakingly beautiful. Coming into Guadalajara Airport, I could see the roadways were profuse with wild flowers and thought, "Some things about this assignment are going to be good."

The twenty minute drive from Guadalajara Airport took me past tiny villages and many fields of corn. Cows and horses ambled across the road, occasionally bringing the cab to a stop. The last five minutes of the trip we were climbing gentle hills.

The two lane roadway curved around and over until from the top I could again see Lake Chapala. From my vantage point the water looked like a small ocean, the breeze causing gentle waves.

The village of Chapala hugged the edge of the lake and nestled between it and surrounding hills. We reached a turn off a short distance before coming into Chapala. Soon we were at my destination, the village of Ajijic. The cab stopped at a quaint, charming hotel which had been part of a convent during the fifteenth century.

Checking in, I thought of my father and how much he would enjoy researching the history of this place. The hotel was quaint but the present owners had brought it up to date as far as plumbing and the big spacious kitchen. They had retained the feel of the fifteenth century by furnishing it with that period, using hand woven fabrics and antiques. It had a five star rating, rare in this locale.

I had a suite reserved that overlooked the lake and mountains on the other side. Below me in the courtyard were various trees, banana, orange, lime, and papaya. Flowers of red, yellow, purple and pink, complimented the trees. A smile found me and suddenly I felt at peace for the first time in many a day. My love for Mexico had sparked.

Later as I walked alone beside the lake, trying to get a feel for the village, the sunset was spectacular. Mexicans I met while walking seemed unusually friendly. I kept my Spanish language skills to myself, stumbling over *"Buenas tardes."*

The village was small. Leaving the beach, I walked toward the church steeple knowing I'd find the plaza and center of all activity. Heavy trees provided deep shade on the plaza. A guitar player strolled around the square, strumming and looking for possible contributions. With a jaunt in my step I walked back to the hotel. It was time for me to go into the hotel lounge and lay my act in front of the foreigners gathered there for the cocktail hour.

Surprisingly, there was a scattering of affluent looking Mexicans among them. I wondered if any of them were involved in the drug trafficking. It would be part of my job, to investigate. It didn't take long to get invited to a table by a man and woman having drinks. Every eye was on me, the newcomer in town. My self-appointed host and hostess had been living in the area for a few years and were very informative.

As I sat down, I told them how grateful I was to be invited over. I let them think I was rather nervous about being outside the United States and in a foreign country. They were forthcoming about who they were and what they were about. Bill told me, "I'm a minister by profession and so is Nancy." Nancy mentioned that they were doing seminars on how to become an ordained minister.

At that moment I realized I had probably been invited over as a likely prospect for their seminars. I was quick to tell them that I was a school teacher from Iowa. I told them I had taught third and fourth grades and was pretty much burned out on teaching.

"In the teaching process, I have discovered a shortage of books geared toward the elementary age group," I said, "and I have taken a sabbatical to try my hand at writing." It worked well. They even told me they had a niece who taught.

We sat there through happy hour and they invited me to continue through dinner with them. I accepted, apologizing for seeming so eager. As the evening progressed I was amazed at their agility with the Spanish language. Their accent wasn't that good but they seemed to have an extensive vocabulary and be a very popular couple. During and after dinner, several people strolled over to say hello and talk about the much discussed seminars on religion.

One of the people who dropped by was a striking women named Liz Byrnes. She was very articulate, with an air of authority about her. It didn't take long for me to realize that she was probably the social lioness of Ajijic. She informed me she had retired from a supervisory position in some government agency. She had married into money and they had retired and come to Mexico to live. Her husband died, soon after their move to Ajijic, of a prolonged illness, prostate cancer. She was having a party, in a few days, and of course I was invited to attend. She seemed eager to include me as a part of her group.

Soon after she left us, two men came over and pulled up chairs. They were a pair of homosexuals: the older one agringo and the younger a quite handsome Mexican man. They didn't stay long but during the time they were there they let me know they were homosexuals and had been together for twelve years. I calculated the Mexican man to be about twenty-seven. I wasn't too shocked by this. In Greece where I had my last assignment, it was a very common occurrence. Some Greeks have their wife (for family), their mistress (for fun), and their young boy (for sex).

After they saw I wasn't shocked, and some rather desultory conversation about the weather, they excused themselves and moved over to another table with more overt homosexuals. There seemed to be quite a few of them in the dining area.

I discussed my plans to rent a small house, hopefully with a garden. Bill told me of one right on the beach. Several other alternatives were given but my mind stayed on the one he described as "right on the beach."

When dinner was served I realized how hungry I was. A light lunch had been served on the plane but hours had passed. A tall, thin Mexican boy, of maybe sixteen years, brought us shrimp prepared in a spicy sauce along with bowls of steaming rice and vegetables. Mexican bread, a small crusty roll called a *bolillo*, was served last, along with sweet butter. After dinner, another drink, and a few more questions of my host and hostess, I excused myself and left with Liz's phone number in my hand. I needed to be up early for house hunting.

Up at sunrise, I decided to walk west on the beach. After only five minutes of walking I came upon a small blue, glass fronted house with a fenced front yard and a for rent sign hanging on the gate, there was a telephone number. I memorized the number and continued my walk. "What a great place to go horseback riding," I told myself.

Another few minutes down the beach, I came upon the estate I had seen in photographs in Washington. It was enclosed by a high fence and occupied two city blocks of space. In addition to the fence, it was walled on three sides, leaving only the beach side visible through the wire fence. It appeared to have everything, boat ramp, green houses, and stables for horses, barely visible through the fence and thick trees. The pictures did not do it justice. The entire beach front of the two story house was glass. Guests must have had a terrific view of the lake.

Leaving my looking for another day, I jogged back to the hotel thinking I would call and make an appointment to see the little blue house. I was wrong. Things move slowly in Mexico.

The realtor's phone was out of order so I put my walking shoes back on and started out again. I was lucky the village was small. When the realtor and I finally got together to walk through the house, I thought it perfect and couldn't believe my luck.

It was right on the lake, one story, one bedroom that opened into a lovely garden filled with bougainvillea, roses, lilies, and even a banana tree loaded with fruit. It had adequate kitchen facilities with fairly new appliances, a small room that could be used as a den and a glass fronted, floor to ceiling, large room that would serve as my living and dining room. A double fireplace opened into the living room and den. The house had everything, including a maid and a gardener three days a week. The one drawback was no telephone but it was my understanding that few houses in the village had one. It wasn't difficult to get moved in and settled.

On a more sober thought, I remembered the large estate where a drug lord might be hiding, just a few minutes down the beach.

It was simple to break into the social scene. Almost any newcomer was like a breath of fresh air. The expatriates saw too much of each other. They welcomed any diversion. I met several people through Bill and Nancy, the couple with whom I dined on my first night in the village.

I found most of the people I met either bored or boring. The medium age was fifty five, with a small smattering of younger, retiree, drop outs, among them some very wealthy former dope dealers.

Drugs were rampant at almost any party you attended, with a choice of various kinds of pot: Le Tai from Hawaii, Acapulco Gold, Colombian, homegrown and Chapala Chartreuse. There was always a small bowl of coke with spoon and plenty of alcohol.

I could see it was going to be a difficult assignment. I would have to have plenty of excuses from the social scene to find time for work. As far as I had been able to figure out, the few token Mexicans invited into foreign homes were connections for the foreigners to purchase drugs. Some of them had become very rich but they acted bored with the foreigners. The Mexican connections were the local variety not anywhere near the international level I was looking for. They were mainly suppliers for the locals and foreigners who used drugs.

After a week or so of being here, I had decided it was like that island in Scotland where everyone was a smuggler. They smuggled Scotch into England tax free. Everyone knew everyone was doing it, but no one talked about it. It seemed to be what was happening in Ajijic. Not on a large scale but several were making their little deals, packing out their RVs and boats, driving them across the border themselves or getting a mule. With pot going for two hundred dollar an ounce, it didn't take too long to get rich. I hoped this fast crowd I had become acquainted with, would lead me into what I came to find, but I doubted it.

2

THE MEETING

Fate was soon to take my hand. I had become enamored with riding early in the morning. I had made friends with one of the guys who rented horses. When he saw I was a good rider and faithful about it, he allowed me to ride his own personal horse. He was a sixteen and a half hand-high jumper named Vesuvio. El Pequeño, the horse owner, had taught himself to ride, jump and train horses. Vesuvio could do everything, jump, dance, back up, count and wiggle his ears on command. Bright and early he would bring the horse by for me to ride, sometimes riding with me on another horse he called Cinco de Mayo. He usually left the horse with me so I could ride alone.

I rode west on the beach each morning, so the morning sun wouldn't be in my eyes. I always rode by the big estate I mentioned earlier. Sometimes slowing down and peering through the fence. There was something about the estate that fascinated me, beyond my assignment.

I had unconsciously gotten into a routine. I never planned for my pleasant excursions to put me in danger. One morning, a month or so after my arrival in Ajijic, I rode west as usual down the beach. When the estate appeared in the near distance, I again wondered about my fascination for this place. It was weird. I knew what was probably behind the fences and walls, but I didn't feel fear looking at it. I pulled up to the fence and got off once again. The garden visible through the fence looked like a fairy land. Water from the sprinklers clung to roses of every color, trees gracefully draped over white wrought iron benches. I was so enchanted I never saw the big black car pull behind me until it stopped.

Two huge Mexican men got out and slammed me against the fence and asked in angry tones what I was doing there. I kept my cool. Their move was to lead my horse off toward the garden gate and I was shoved into their car and driven through another gate. At the house, I was taken out of the car and lead up to a *terraza*.

Sitting on the *terraza* was one of the handsomest of men. He was one of the drug lords I had been sent down to find: Enrique Vázquez. The two bodyguards led me up to him. I could only think that my cover had been blown and I was about to have the same thing happen to me.

My mind flashed back to the dossier I had seen on Enrique Vázquez when he had first been brought to the attention of the DEA. It was his first interaction with one of the drug lords in Columbia. He had set up a deal for a Miami connect for five hundred pounds of coke, a relatively small deal in Columbia. While bringing this deal down, there had been a few days of partying and telling 'Can you top this?' stories. The story telling had gotten out of hand and some of them had made the dealers suspicious of the Miami connect. In fact, even Enrique had gotten suspicious, but he was willing to give him the benefit of the doubt. According to the dossier, they couldn't confirm the stories. The Miami connect was found dead of a drug overdose in a hotel in Medellin.

Enrique had gotten into drug dealing on a large scale through his contacts with the pharmaceutical company that belonged to his family. Some of the Colombian warlords had been his college buddies, also from wealthy families. That little tidbit I had read in the dossier made me know that I would probably have to do one of my best acting jobs ever.

I was recalling the misconception that most people have of dope smugglers. The popular concept is that they are all kept drug addicts. This may have been true years ago but our files are full of people that you would never suspect. Most of them looked like "old money rich." The giveaway was that they acted "nouveau riche." Knowing all this, I didn't doubt that he could, and would, kill if his personal safety or his drug operation was involved. He and his Colombian partners contributed large sums of money to prevent prosecution. They also helped the economy of the countries they lived in and the United States on a very large scale. This was why it was so hard to stop.

Enrique Vázquez sat at a table; an appetizing breakfast set before him. He glanced up at me with cold black angry eyes.

"What's so interesting about my house? I've watched you on several occasions and you always ride slow, looking in this direction. Sometimes you even get off your horse and peer through my fence." He picked up his fork, took a bite of egg, and looked up at me again, waiting for an answer.

"Look," I said, "I didn't see you. If I had I would have spoken."

His eyes never left my face as he ordered me to produce some identification. "I suspect you are a foreigner," he said in a deep threatening voice. "I'm sure you wouldn't like me to telephone the police."

My training stood me in good stead. I gave nothing away. I had been busted by a routine. I knew better. However, I could not have planned this meeting any better. All at once I was this indignant Midwestern school teacher, a citizen of the United States, being treated like a criminal.

"How dare you, you inconsiderate bum?" I yelled. "I may have you and your personal goons arrested for abducting me. I am a citizen of the United States, a visitor in your country. Is this the way you treat visitors who admire your lovely home? I'm leaving and you better not try to stop me."

I heard him laughing as I crossed the grass to a side gate.

"Where's my horse?" I yelled back at him.

The fact that I was badly shaken worked in my favor. When he stood up from the table I could see he was tall and trim. He spoke briefly to one of the men and then walked down the steps and came across the grass toward me. I wanted to run but I knew if I wanted to get to know him, I would have to stand my ground. As he came closer, I suddenly became aware of a new feeling. There was a sexual tension between us.

"Your horse will be brought around," he told me. "If you are who you say you are, I may teach you how to ride."

Glaring at him, I replied, "Don't hold your breath."

Knees shaking, I turned and walked toward the man leading my horse.

I was so unnerved by my unexpected encounter with the wanted drug lord that I spent the rest of that day in my little house. There seemed to be no way to plan my activities in this assignment. Events seemed to plan themselves. First, this house right down the beach from him had conveniently been for rent. Second, a meeting that I had planned to arrange was arranged for me.

"Where do I go from here?" I wondered as I ate a solitary dinner.

The next morning I was awake before dawn. The weather was warm and inviting. I hurriedly drank a glass of guava juice and walked to the house of El Pequeño, located east down the beach from me. His wife, Leonora, was in the kitchen and called to him to get out of bed.

"You owe me, *señorita*," he smiled as I rode away on Vesuvio.

East was my direction today. I couldn't face the west so soon after yesterday. Fishermen were casting off in their little boats. Lights were visible in some of the houses. I rode slowly enjoying the early dawn.

After a few minutes I heard the loud fast sound of hoofs pounding the sand. In the near distance I could see a black stallion coming toward me in a full run. The rider hadn't seen me and the horse was nearly upon me. My horse veered toward the water. Only experience and a good horse kept me in the saddle. The stallion and rider flew by me before the rider could bring the huge animal to a stop. Turning the stallion around, the rider brought the horse alongside mine.

When he saw who it was, Enrique said, breathing fast, "You evidently do need riding lessons. Don't you know better than to ride in front of a racing horse?"

Before I could answer or knew what was happening, he leaned toward me and swept me off my horse with one arm, pulling me up to him with the other. He kissed me cruelly on the mouth and then let me slide down the side of the stallion until my feet touched the ground.

"You scared the shit out of me," he growled. "I could have killed you."

With that he rode off again thundering toward his own property. Surprised and stunned, I stood where he had left me and stared in his direction until he was out of sight. My fury had been extinguished, sexual attraction had replaced it. Evidently, it wasn't one-sided. I walked my horse slowly back. I needed to get my adrenalin back to normal.

"Take a deep breath. Go slow," I told myself. "Keep your mind on the assignment. This guy is the enemy."

Later that afternoon when I was safely back in my house, the doorbell rang. Shea, a florist, was delivering to me, conservatively, about two hundred orchids, along with a big basket of goodies, a jeroboam of champagne, Beluga caviar, smoked oysters, English crackers, Greek olives, five cheeses and an invitation to dine with Enrique later that evening in Guadalajara. His enclosed note apologized for his rude behavior.

I didn't want him to think I'd been waiting to hear from him, so I declined. The agent was playing it cool as trained. The fascinated woman in me was thrilled that he wanted my company. I sent a brief note accepting his apology, but telling him I would have to decline because I was committed to a party in the village.

That evening I took great care dressing for my night out. I wore a vivid red chiffon dress with a flared skirt and a flattering neckline.

It was good that I did. Enrique had gotten himself invited to the party. The locals were in shock: it was his first social appearance. Liz Byrnes' season was made. She had had the honor of getting this mysterious person, the one who had bought the ex-governor's house, to come out socially.

Her party was a success. I realized this a few minutes after he arrived. I was flattered that he came, but I knew the role I was playing required me to be friendly but distant. Ajijic had its number of single women, most of them affluent, through death or divorce. Fortunately for me, their medium age was probably fifty five. Many of them looked and acted much, much younger. A lot of them had some help from a plastic surgeon.

I didn't feel any threats from them. They certainly didn't feel threatened by me, a little Midwest school teacher, who was on a limited budget, and supposedly outside the continental United States to write children's books. Those boring, frustrated women were all over him, but his eyes sought only mine. He was trying to be attentive and polite to them.

I sauntered over to Tom and Tony, the two gays I had met previously at the Posada. They were talking about Enrique's appearance and wanted to know if I knew him, and where we had met. Not wanting to tell them about my traumatic experience with his body guards, I told them we had met while walking on the beach. I told them I was also surprised to see him there and I agreed with them that he was quite a hunk. I had gotten out of Enrique's range of vision and he was excusing himself and moving where he could see me. The tension between us seemed so obvious; it amazed me that others didn't seem to notice it.

As previously stated, I was no slouch in the looks department, and I was getting my share of attention. It was apparent he was getting antsy, so I strolled over and joined the group he was talking with. Liz started to introduce us, and he said, "We've met." Liz obviously saw me as her protégée, and was taken aback that I had already met Enrique. She was a take charge type of woman and had these categories in which to place each person.

Enrique seemed so pleased that at last I was at his side. He leaned over and whispered in my ear, "I will never again appreciate red on another woman. The color is yours."

I couldn't let him know how strong I felt the attraction.

We stayed together laughing and talking with the other guests for about an hour. After that I excused myself, thanked my hostess and left. I had to get away. He was SO drop dead gorgeous; I was getting wrapped up in my mental picture. Time out was necessary for me to remember what I was here to accomplish.

The next morning I was up early and riding east on the beach so I wouldn't be riding past the estate. I don't think he outguessed me. Looking back, I think he had my house staked out. Anyway, he found me riding up through the village toward the mountains. It was so beautiful. Adjectives like verdant, lush, tropical and colorful come to mind. One of the many reasons this area was populated with so many foreigners was the climate, gentle people, and the beauty of it all.

As he rode up to me, I wondered what Enrique found so interesting in this area. We had a long ride into the mountains; the sun was up in the sky by the time we got back to the village, where we went to the La Posada for a mid-morning brunch.

I had found out many things about him. He had kept pretty much to the truth, according to the dossier I had seen on him prior to coming here. He was the only son of a prominent family from Monterey. His father had owned a pharmaceutical company and he inherited from his father. It was one of the largest in Mexico. They had many American contacts as well as in Central and South America. This fact alone gave them the ability to travel at will, to anywhere they wished to go. He had attended a small Catholic Military Academy in Texas as a child. He had graduated from Stanford University with honors as a political science major. His father's dying wish was for him to become president of Mexico.

He told me he was here in the village to hang out, that he was burned out and didn't know exactly what he wanted to do with the rest of his life. He had taken on the responsibility of the Pacific Coast area for the company. He stated he had twenty or more people working directly under him and offices in Guadalajara.

I went along with everything I was told, acting naive and impressed. He told me he was married to someone he didn't love, that she had been selected for him by his family. He said that other than family background they had nothing in common. "She is a spoiled brat," he said, "whose father gives her everything she wants and she wants everything." He said they had two children, a boy and a girl. His wife, according to him, spent most of her time traveling in Europe and the children were being raised by nannies. His mother might drop in once or twice a week to check on them but she is more or less like his wife, real heavy into the social scene and traveling.

I was a good listener. I really had him talking all through the ride back down the mountain. Our rhythm was broken once we got off our horses.

There were a few of the party goers from last night gathered to have brunch at the Posada. I could see that everyone at the table was shocked to see us enter the dining room together.

Liz, our hostess from the night before, could hardly wait to get me alone for questioning. She had designated herself as my social secretary. Here I was doing things on my own. She hadn't figured out yet where Enrique could fit into her social scheming, or whether she could manipulate him as she did the others. We went through a question and answer period by our brunch companions. I had my story well-rehearsed, and I could see that Enrique was good at dissembling also. He told nothing that couldn't be checked out if someone went to the trouble.

Everyone had cute stories to tell about themselves or someone they knew, about their ability to communicate in Spanish.

One that I thought hilarious was about the woman who asked the maid to wash the refrigerator with *sopa*, thinking that *sopa* meant soap. She came home to find the refrigerator covered in red tomato soup, *sopa* being the word for soup. It seems so illogical that a maid would do that but they think all *gringos* are crazy. This led to someone asking if I spoke Spanish, and I told them that I had about six hours of college Spanish. I said that I hadn't practiced it at all but sometimes could get a glimmer of what was being said. Enrique joked that he was going to be my private tutor while I was in Mexico.

After twenty or thirty minutes of this superficial conversation (almost everyone being hung over), we excused ourselves and went to another table. Enrique asked if he could order for me. He ordered us a fresh fruit plate and *chilaquiles*. The fruit was at its peak. The *chilaquiles* were an experience.

Chilaquiles are the Mexican way of utilizing day old tortillas. The tortillas are cut in strips and fried until crisp. They are then covered in a mild red chili sauce and served with grated cheese, onion and sour cream. Exquisite!

He explained that they used to be considered something that only the very poor ate. One of Mexico's presidents had made them popular among the upper crust and they had become the 'in thing' to order. While we were discussing food, culture, etcetera, he invited me to go with him the next day to Guadalajara.

This was yet another opportunity to find out what he was all about, and maybe get a lead on something to do with the reason I was here.

I said, "Yes of course."

There wasn't much point in letting him think I was shy. I would play the school teacher until I believed it myself. He had ordered some small boys to take care of the horses. They had rubbed them down and were awaiting his orders. They walked the horses home and we walked along the lake back to my house and then he to his.

He wanted to see me for dinner but I begged off using the altitude, the party, and horseback riding as an excuse that I was very tired. We parted with a date to leave for Guadalajara at eight thirty the following day. I was glad to have some time by myself.

Things were moving so fast and I certainly had not expected my protagonist to be such a charming, refined person. I needed this afternoon and evening to get my thoughts together. The remainder of the day I spent in unpacking, thinking of my modus operandi and what I would wear on my trip tomorrow.

3

GUADALAJARA

After a delightful night's sleep, I arose to find a basket of fresh fruit on my doorstep, along with a single white rose. I decided I would wear the Galion design that I had picked up in one of the local boutiques. The sales girl had told me this designer was famous on a national level. I could see why; the costume I had bought was so original in design and flavor. She had taken the best of Mexico and incorporated it into this dress. Nothing garish. She had used the subtle earth tones and natural fibers to make a master piece of design.

Yes, I was thinking, this will impress Enrique. It will be perfect for a day in the city.

I was dressed and waiting for Enrique, eager to see Guadalajara. He escorted me to his house where a helicopter awaited us. I wasn't disappointed. As we were walking to the helicopter he commented on my dress. He seemed surprised when I told him it was Galion design, Mexican label, and I had bought it in a boutique in Ajijic the day before. He seemed pleased that I had bought something new to please him. The ego of men! I had bought it to please myself.

Our first stop was landing on the roof of his office building on Chapultepec Avenue. There were guards on the roof which brought back to me memories of what drug money could do and the point of my being here. The office was plush and there was no doubt as to who was boss. We had coffee and croissants in the executive dining room and after Enrique gave orders for the day we were off to see Guadalajara.

We visited the José Clemente Orozco Museum, named after one of Mexico's great muralists that lived and painted during the early nineteen hundreds. After that we went to Hospicio Cabañas, which at one time was an orphans' home, through the Cathedral, government offices, governor's palace and the Degollado Theater.

Our last stop was the San Juan de Dios Market. Such an array of merchandise I had never seen before. There was one section of fresh fruits and vegetables, each stall piled high with fruit polished until they looked like jewels. The vegetables were the very freshest, brought in just a few hours before from the surrounding villages.

There was another section of just flowers, fresh ones and also some made of paper. The imagination of the Mexican knows no bounds when it comes to flower making, some of the paper ones looked as if they were real. Another section had clothes, shoes and other leather goods, pottery and jewelry. I really wanted to shop but kept myself in check because I knew he would want to buy things for me.

When we left the market Enrique led me over to horse driven carriages called a *calandria*. These were used in the eighteen hundreds. They were now used as tourist gimmicks in front of the Market. We entered a *calandria* and were driven to the Quinta Real for lunch.

There is something to be said about being very rich, the only word that comes to mind is, "Wow'. This is one of Guadalajara's few five star hotels. It was very impressive, with waiters in white gloves; they were unusually attentive. As a general rule, I prefer a more informal type of eating arrangement but this was a real treat.

While having lunch, Enrique asked if I would go with him to Morelia the following day. I couldn't pretend. In for a penny, in for a pound, so of course I said, "*Si.*"

After a long lunch we went to the shopping center nearest the hotel. He wanted me to get a feel of what the city was like for shopping, etc. Two tired people went back to the office, boarded the helicopter, and back to the lake. I begged off again about dinner saying that I wanted to get ready for the Morelia trip.

The next day I awoke to the maid arriving with an arm load of red roses, a note attached asking me if I was ready to fly to Morelia. I couldn't believe it was going to be this easy. It seemed right away that I was being accepted. I was wary but I also wanted to see him, the sexual attraction we had must play itself out.

With the Latin male, as with most men, the whole sexual thing is conquest. In my limited experience I had been amazed at the great length a man will go to get you into his bed. This being the ultimate goal, the longer you can keep him out of it the more involved he wants to get.

Self-control being one of my strong points, I had to plan carefully. It was a dangerous, exciting game I was playing. My life was on the line at all times. When you are in a covert drug operation you have no way of knowing who is double dealing who. Your constant prayer is that no one blows your cover.

I sent him a note telling him I'd be ready within the hour and that I needed to know if we were going to be gone overnight. His reply informed me it was only two hours by plane to Morelia but his business might keep him until the late afternoon. He wrote that he had made reservations at "Las Mañanitas." This is a famous small hotel in Morelia that had at one time been an old hacienda. An American bought it and turned it into a hotel. I believed Enrique could write a book about all of the quaint, charming hotels in Mexico.

4

MORELIA

We left around 11.00am and flew over some beautiful stately mountains. I was in awe of the Lear jet. It seated ten people and was luxurious, cold, icy champagne to drink en route. I was impressed again when we arrived in Morelia. In spite of his being on a business trip, he had arranged to have a mariachi band waiting our arrival. It was not that the mariachi were there that impressed me, it was the number of them, twenty in all, and the way they were dressed: immaculate white suits, silver buttons, and white sombreros.

There was also a waiting chauffeur-driven limousine to take us to the hotel. First we were driven through the city. Most of the buildings of the town of Morelia are made of pink sandstone. At sunset the city glows in these pink and gold colors. It is said one of Mexico's presidents, Morelos, was born of an Indian woman on the sidewalk outside of the municipal market. If true, she chose a good, although primitive place. The beauty of the lighting in late evening would have taken her mind off the pain.

Our bags were taken into the hotel. We freshened up and went into the bar for a drink. While having the drink, Enrique gave me a choice of going with him to an hacienda where he had a business appointment or staying in my suite.

I really agonized about what to do but decided it would be less suspicious if I elected to stay in the suite. After we finished our drink he left me there.

I had made a wise choice. He left one of his *guardaespaldas* (bodyguards) to keep me in cold champagne and the fire going in the fireplace. He stood guard outside my door until Enrique returned. Enrique arrived in a jovial mood. He said things had gone well but he would be going back in the morning. He explained to me that the hacienda he had visited was from the sixteenth century and very beautiful. He wanted me to go with him the next day so that I could see it.

A phone call produced the limousine again and we were taken to the plaza to walk around. Enrique bought me a hand-woven rebozo, and a pair of gold filigree earrings. It was difficult to refuse the gifts.

Later over dinner, he made several veiled references to our sharing my suite. He had the mariachi sing me a song about this man who went into the city to sell his produce and found this rebozo of beautiful colors. This made him think of his wife. Although he couldn't afford it, he bought it anyway. There was no sacrifice too great for his wife.

The song was beautiful in sentiment and I was falling in love. There were many songs of love that night. At one point, he stood and sang a song to me. The song is called 'El Rogán'. It comes from the verb *rogar* which means ... damn, it's difficult to translate and get the true meaning. In the case of the song, it is when you want something badly, let's say another person, and they keep saying "No, no, no," but you persist until you win them over to you. Then you are called El Rogán, as in the song. He had a beautiful singing voice and the words to the song were romantic and provocative.

I was almost persuaded but knew I must keep my head and keep him at arm's length, at least until I could find out what he was really into. We finally tore ourselves away from each other and went to our separate rooms. We had agreed to have breakfast in my suite at ten o'clock the next day.

After a sleepless night, I was up at eight thirty trying to repair the damage done to my face by lack of sleep. I put on my most flattering, enchanting peignoir. I opened the door to a big bouquet of mixed flowers, a small box tied to them. It was a beautiful gold chain I had admired while he was buying the earrings. I loved it.

Following a leisurely breakfast, we left the hotel for the hacienda. It was about thirty kilometers from Morelia, much further than I expected. I could sense immediately that something clandestine was going on. It wasn't what anyone said, or the way they were acting, it was just a feel that I have for such things. It probably has to do with my training. It was obviously a pig farm. There must have been about three thousand pigs. There were signs posted everywhere saying, "Do not enter unless authorized."

I asked Enrique what the signs were. He told me that pigs are susceptible to disease, especially *triquinosis*, or trichinosis as we know it. This disease kills many people, mostly children, in Mexico each year as most people raise their own pigs. Enrique said the Mexican government was trying to eradicate the disease and that was the reason for the signs.

The signs had a dual purpose: they kept people out and allowed the clandestine drug operation that was going on to be unobserved. I was later to learn that besides being a pig farm, it was a laboratory. Several sheds used for sorting marijuana were guarded by Mexican soldiers.

That day I was treated royally, as was Enrique. His host had arranged a real Mexican fiesta. The patio area was decorated with paper cutouts in all colors. They had a *ballet folklórico* and mariachi band. A special barbecue, a whole pig rubbed down with spices, wrapped in maguey leaves, put in a pit filled with coals from the mesquite bush and baked overnight, had been prepared. It was my first time to try it and I found it finger-licking good.

There was a smattering of women, some obviously maids and cooks, but there were several I couldn't figure out. They were mostly well groomed and well dressed, but I sensed that they were "on loan," or maybe window dressing. I saw no official hostess. Perhaps the wife of the owner was away or kept out of sight on these business parties.

One thing for sure, the other women couldn't figure me out, probably didn't want to. They probably thought I was a *gringa puta* that Enrique had picked up in Morelia. I could see what they couldn't understand was the tenderness and respect he was showing me. Not that anyone was disrespectful to them, but there was a palpable difference. We all had a good time. During the fun time Enrique excused himself and took care of what I assumed was business.

Early in the evening we returned to Morelia. Over a quiet cup of coffee in the hotel, Enrique asked me if I would like to fly on to Pátzcuaro. I agreed and we went upstairs, again to our separate rooms.

Mexico was so exciting seeing it through the eyes of a beloved Mexican. I was really thrilled about going to Pátzcuaro on Mexico's second largest lake. I had read an article about it in *National Geographic* magazine. Although I have been a world traveler, I hadn't traveled much in Mexico. As we flew over the lake early the next day, it was breathtaking to see the boats with their butterfly nets of various colors rowing out for three days of fishing.

Pátzcuaro's largest population is made up of Tarascan Indians, who still maintain much of their culture, especially in the way the women dress with brightly embroidered layers of skirts. They wear smocked blouses mostly made of satin, with their rebozos and handwoven baskets containing their days shopping or the handmade things they have for sale.

Some of the men still dress in native costume also, the white *manta* wrap around pants, embroidered shirts, *serape* and *huaraches*, the same type of clothing that was used during the time of Pancho Villa. Seeing these can take you right back to the history books.

They made quite a picture. The women waiting on the shore were interspersed with a gaggle of children and men, most of them in their native dress, and of course the usual bunch of goats, chickens, and yapping dogs. It all made for a folkloric, picturesque, unforgettable impression.

Enrique loved Mexico and saw it all through the eyes of love. I too was beginning to see Mexico through the eyes of love, not only for the land, but for the man beside me. I was trying desperately to remember I was here on a mission.

The public market was a letdown after the spectacular landing. Enrique bought me another beautiful rebozo and a peasant blouse. We went to Don Vasco's Hotel for breakfast. I waited there reading a book while Enrique took care of some business. He very carefully explained that it had to do with his pharmaceutical company. The fact that he explained made me immediately more curious. His meeting didn't last long, maybe forty-five minutes.

We went back to the plane and took off again, this time for Santa Clara del Cobre. As we were flying over Santa Clara del Cobre, I was thinking about some of the things I had read in Washington about how, in these areas of high elevation, many people grow marijuana and poppies. I had read how it is a cash crop for most of them. They even have clandestine laboratories where they refine the poppies.

Although the hashish is not considered the world's best, the *goma* (as the finished poppy product is called in Mexico) is considered some of the best, and the cause of many deaths and addiction because of its strength. It is sometimes hard to come to terms with the beauty you are seeing, knowing below you there are laboratories of death.

Santa Clara del Cobre is a little copper mining town that is famous for its copper products. The designs there are primitive, but have won many prizes internationally. I wanted everything I saw and wasn't disappointed. Enrique practically bought out the town for me: copper bracelets, earrings, big bells, little bells, candelabra, and some really extraordinary vases and pots. It was Christmas every day being with him.

On our way back to Morelia we took the opportunity to fly over the volcanoes and to see the monarch butterflies that I had casually mentioned I would like to see. I don't know how it looked on the ground, but from the air there were butterflies clinging to trees, houses, rocks and anything else they could find. I had also read about these butterflies in *National Geographic*. It seems they migrate each year to this area and it has become a national and international event to come and see them.

Late in the afternoon we returned to Morelia, packed our bags and flew back to Ajijic. I didn't want to leave him and I could see he felt the same way. He begged me to stay with him, but my good training took over and I declined. So far I hadn't broken any rules, but I knew I was getting close. The constant turmoil was how could I get out of it, knowing there was no way out? I would have to play it to the bitter end of my assignment, and I knew, suffer consequences.

We couldn't stay away from each other. Every day we went horseback riding, met for cocktails or took long walks through the village, laughing and talking. After a few days of this, he asked me if I would like to go to Mexico City. He said he had an American business associate he was meeting there. He told me that after his meeting in Mexico City he wanted to take me to see the Pyramids. Here was another chance to find out what I could about his business, also if I were honest, another chance to be with him.

5

MEXICO CITY

I stayed at El Presidente in the presidential suite. He had a condo in the Zona Rosa, not too far from the hotel. He and his business partner would be staying there. I had the usual bodyguard outside my room, who went with me when I went out. I was allowed to shop but not allowed to pay for anything. It kind of inhibited my shopping.

Mexico City is a teeming metropolis and one of the most beautiful cities in the world, with its blend of Indian and European culture, the fountains, tall buildings, and museums. I enjoyed the city if not my shopping.

I didn't think there was a chance that I would get to meet this American. Enrique had told me that the American was a Texan and that they had been business partners for several years in a chain of pharmacies in Texas. They had gone to the same military school and at one time he had been a strong candidate as a brother-in-law. He had gone on to tell me that he felt Texans, generally speaking, had a strong prejudice against Mexicans. He was kind of shamefaced when he admitted that he himself had always felt that he should marry someone of his own culture.

I hadn't thought of him in terms of marriage, but for me he was admitting that he was also prejudiced. He could sense he had hurt me by this remark. I was hoping to maybe overhear bits and pieces over the telephone or things he told the bodyguard. When he came to check on me that night he asked if I would like to have lunch with him and his business partner the next day.

I didn't think there was a chance that his partner would know me, or that I would know him. I had dressed carefully, wanting Enrique to be proud of me and suspecting that was why he wanted me to meet his partner. Coming down in the elevator Enrique told me we would be having lunch in a private dining room.

Enrique was smiling and happy as he introduced me. Imagine my surprise when his partner turned out to be the governor of Texas. I could hardly believe that he was involved in drugs. I began to believe that maybe they did have some legitimate business dealings. When the governor asked Enrique how the Morelia meeting had gone, I knew how deep it was getting.

After lunch and back at the hotel, I bought every American newspaper I could find, but couldn't find any reference to the governor of Texas being in Mexico for any reason. I was frightened, and concerned. This assignment seemed to be getting bigger and more involved.

He certainly must have the ability and resources to find out about me if he took the trouble. I could only pray that Andrew had me well hidden in the DEA.

I had certainly put on my best Midwestern school teacher act, acting really impressed but also kind of vague, like I couldn't be sure what was happening and didn't much care. When he had attempted to engage me in the conversation, I would dissimulate and start talking about shopping and museums. I asked if he had seen the Chapultepec Palace. I acted like a complete airhead. I hoped I hadn't overdone it as Enrique looked at me speculatively several times. I was hoping he would think I was acting this way because I was overwhelmed by meeting the governor.

After that luncheon ordeal, the *guardaespalda* and I took off to see the Chapultepec Palace. I was excited about seeing it. That period in Mexico had been rather turbulent. I knew very little about the actual history of it all, but I did know that Carlota had been much maligned and hated by the Mexicans because of her extravagance, as I recalled. She had made quite a splash socially and had been indiscreet romantically, but had ended up owning this palace that I was about to see. I should mention in passing that she was sent back to France in a straightjacket or its equivalent for those times.

The castle was rather primitive as compared to the European castles of the same period, but after all Mexico was not too far from that era when the Aztec were ripping out the hearts of their enemies and eating them while they were still beating. In spite of the violence in this period, women were involved and interested in jewels and clothing. Carlota seemed to have had her fair share of both. She had some really beautiful pieces. I was fascinated by a little beaded purse that looked so much like one that had been in my family for a long time.

After the Palace we caught a cab to the Museum of Anthropology where I spent the afternoon wandering around looking at Pre Columbian art, with Miguel trailing along with me. I had gotten used to Miguel, my *guardaespalda*. It seemed he was always with me.

I was thinking of that word bodyguard and how it implies a certain kind of intimacy. Miguel and I had kept it impersonal, but the Museum of Anthropology humanized him for me. Anthropology had been one of his majors in College so he had a knowledgeable interest in seeing it. It was exciting for me. I knew enough to keep him talking about the different periods. Although he volunteered very little of his personal life, at that time, he would do so later. He certainly made me aware of the complexity of the Mexican culture.

Even though I enjoyed Miguel's company, I had to talk to Enrique about this. I had no room to move. My logic when I talked to him would be, after all, I'm a nobody. I didn't need a bodyguard and further I didn't want one; it called attention to me as a foreigner. I thought I already knew his reasons. He didn't want me to get the opportunity to meet another male. Mexican men are among the most possessive males. I would discuss this with him when we next met, which would be early evening when I returned from the museums.

He had to spend some time in his home with his wife and children. I would be having dinner alone in my suite. I had brought along a couple of good books. In fact, I was looking forward to reading them. It helped me to relax and organize my plans. I didn't think it was the proper time to report back about the governor of Texas, but it had surely put me more on guard.

While reading and thinking that evening, there was a knock on the door. It was Miguel with several packages of all sizes and yet another bouquet of flowers. Miguel had also brought me a present, a book on Mexican civilization. I had made a friend and must have somehow impressed him with my limited knowledge about anthropology. Thanking Miguel again as I walked him to the door, I thought to myself, who knows when you may need a friend in a deadly game of chance.

Opening one of the packages, I found a sweet note from Enrique telling me how much in love he was with me, and saying Miguel would check me out of the suite at ten o'clock the next morning and bring me to the airport to meet him. He wrote

that from there we would go to the pyramids. The many packages were perfume, walking boots, socks, riding boots, mine
were rather worn out, I had had them since I was a teenager,
a gorgeous knit sweater, full length leather coat, and a Louis
Vuitton bag to put them in.

Putting the things away, I felt something in the pocket of the
coat. It was a jewelry box, gift wrapped, that contained a gold
bracelet with a little gold charm of the pyramids. He said in the
enclosed note that it couldn't compare to Carlota's jewels, but
he was afraid I wouldn't accept anything more expensive. I was
really getting spoiled. There is something to be said for being a
dope dealer's "babe," money was no object.

Mexico City has an altitude of around 7,500 feet so it
does get cold in the evenings and early mornings. I needed the
leather coat on the way to the airport. The pyramids were awesome, seeing Mexico with a Mexican you can get a whole new
perspective about how young in culture we are as compared to
Mexico. Enrique seemed so proud of his Indian heritage, as well
he should be. Have I mentioned that he was absolutely drop-
dead gorgeous, oh well, I may have repeated myself.

6

ACAPULCO

I don't know if it was planned by him in advance, but after the pyramids we flew to Acapulco. He had a house there and a yacht. After stopping in the town to shop for beach wear for both of us, we went on to the yacht. He also bought me a little gold and emerald macaw for my charm bracelet.

The yacht had a master suite and four state rooms. The dining area on the yacht seated twenty four people. He put me in the master suite with all of my packages and took the one closest to it for himself. On board he had eight employees, besides the bodyguards. He was soon on the phone and people started arriving, mostly men but some were accompanied by women.

I felt that this trip was precipitated by the meeting with the Texas governor. I knew he was definitely setting something up when he introduced me to two Colombians whose pictures I knew well as drug lords.

They were disconcerted but I soon put them at ease by acting as if I wasn't vaguely interested in what was going on. I was reading a book. It seemed I was so innocuous to them, plus they didn't know I spoke Spanish, that they allowed me to stay and read my book while they put the whole deal down on how and where the drop would be for the governor of Texas.

I was scared and jubilant at the same time. My acting lessons had paid off. I had gained Enrique's confidence without sleeping with him, enough so that I sat through that whole plot while reading the book on Mexican civilization that Miguel had given me. Now I was in business, the question to myself was should I notify Andrew now or should I wait to find out some more to give a report?

I could see Enrique's purpose in our shopping before we got to the yacht. This way I had no excuse to go into town. If I should want to, he would insist that someone drive me. I was stuck. I decided to wait for a safer opportunity.

It was party time on the Elena II. Why not? They had just closed a dope deal that would, according to what I overheard, put about three million dollars in Enrique's pockets and probably five million in the pocket of the governor of Texas. Politics at its best, politicians at their best: using their power to line their pockets. Getting that stuff on the street in the good ol' USA so our youth can become mindless and useless and they can control them better – a sinister plot that I hoped with all my heart and soul I would be able to help stop.

More people arrived. As I'm telling this story, I should again comment that you shouldn't see these people in your mind as your conception of the dope dealer. If you saw any one of these people on the yacht that night, you would have thought they were very rich Latin Americans and would never have associated the word dope with them. The newly arrived were dressed in dinner jackets, long gowns, gold chains, flashy rings, mostly in chauffeur driven cars, some with bodyguards.

I dressed with care. I had a pale pink dress that fit like a glove and looked very expensive. I was trying to decide whether to wear my hair up or down when there was a knock on the door.

It was Enrique with a velvet jewel case in his hands and a hang-dog look. The look was because he thought I wouldn't accept his gift. After hearing that deal go down and knowing how much he would make, I felt justified in taking whatever he offered me. I had to graciously accept, maybe protest a little, but not refuse. So, I protested a little and accepted the gift. It was a ruby necklace, earrings and ring, beautiful, the rubies surrounded by diamonds. It would go perfectly with the pink slip dress.

How did he know that? He was one of the most discerning of people. He probably was aware of everything I had in my wardrobe. My wardrobe was limited but good, stylish clothes. I could see I was going to have to improve on it if I was going to maintain this lifestyle. He was thinking along these same lines when he saw me in the dress and rubies.

His comment was, "We have to take you shopping." I didn't demur.

It was time for me to go up on deck and meet his guests. As previously mentioned, there were the Colombian drug lords, whom I had recognized, some minor and not so minor Mexican government officials. One of the officials was from the state of Guerrero. When we were introduced, I thought of what I knew of the state of Guerrero. The cash crop of that state is first marijuana and second tourism. It is also known for growing and refining heroin and because of the high altitude the pot from there is so famous that it is called Acapulco Gold, and among marijuana users is probably one of the most desired on an international level.

My mind was reeling with the impact and magnitude of this drug operation. To all intents and purposes it looked as if it was an ordinary party of the very rich, conducting their business through socializing, which indeed they were.

I knew my report would seem hardly credible and even hesitated to put the whole scene into words, much less written. I was going to be further shocked that night by the arrival, by helicopter, of the governor of Arkansas and his wife. The supper was a buffet served late and in their honor. Enrique told me they were the guests of a Mexican governor. They seemed to be on familiar terms with everyone there.

The governor's wife had a real curiosity about me and I went through a heavy interrogation by her. I acted like an airhead, along for the ride, out to get what I could from Enrique and move on. I did this by bragging about the ruby and diamond jewelry I had on. That popped her eyes out. I hoped again that I was convincing enough that there would be no follow up.

Her significant other also finally got around to me. He had had his eye on me since he came in. I think he saw me as I was projecting and thought he might get a piece for himself. After all, being wanted by a governor is supposed to be impressive. I guess Enrique knew his reputation: he soon put a stop to it, by coming over and putting his hand on my neck. The reader may or may not have noticed but this gesture denotes possession or complete intimacy. In this case it was possession for we had not yet been intimate.

I wasn't privy to what went down between the governor of Arkansas and Enrique but I did see a yacht carrying a Texas flag, two ships down from us. I could only assume it too was loaded out. I was privy to some more information later that bore out my suspicion that they too were involved in smuggling.

Our plans were to fly back to Ajijic the next day. Enrique was entertaining as usual on the trip back, but I felt a reserve I hadn't felt since our relationship began. He served me café latte on the plane and we talked but his thoughts seemed to be elsewhere.

I was happy to be home, so to speak. At least, I was able to be alone. It was mind boggling, the situation I had walked into, and complicated because of what I was feeling for Enrique. Fear was making me more alert. I wondered about his quiet reserve I had felt on the plane. "Don't let it be suspicion," I prayed. It could have been because he had gotten really persistent about our sex life, or I should say our lack of a sex life.

In fact, when we had said goodbye, as he dropped me off, there was a distinct coolness on his part. He informed me that he had some business matters to take care of in Baja California and wouldn't see me for a few days.

I smiled calmly and very carefully explained to him that I might not be home when he got back.

"I'm thinking of visiting my college roommate who lives in Costa Rica," I said, "She's urged me to come for several years and since I'm this close I'd feel bad not going."

He just about went ballistic. I could see his temper rising. I knew he didn't want me gone when he came back, but since he had made his plans he couldn't back down. He had too much pride to ask me not to go. I knew he was beginning to care for me, but I couldn't help but think how the situation would have played if we had already bedded. I was game playing with my life, but my heart was getting much too involved.

7

COSTA RICA

I really did intend to visit a college friend, but I was also planning on meeting Andrew. I had thought it over and decided the things I had to report were too hot to put on the wire or on paper. Andrew's wisdom had gotten me through other assignments and I desperately needed him to bring some sanity back into this one.

I hung around the house for three days and tried to decide what I would report to Andrew, how much of my own feelings I could divulge. I did have some say in the modus operandi but the direction we would take from here depended mostly on what my boss would decide. I didn't believe my supervisors had ever dreamed I would get this close to the situation and be able to come up with all the information that was buzzing around inside my head.

What I really wanted was for Andrew to tell me to pull out. I wanted to come back to Enrique as a regular citizen. I wanted Enrique to be an honest business man. I was dreaming, I would be in it to the bitter end.

It had been several years since I had seen Rosa María and I was looking forward to seeing her again. We had been close friends in college, and she had spent vacations in my home, as I had in hers. She had a handsome brother that I had flirted with for years. He had always seen me as his kid sister's friend. It had lingered in my mind since college to try to change that opinion; I felt disappointed that I wouldn't see him.

Marriage and motherhood was Rosa María's career. She married into a family from Costa Rica. Her husband worked with his family in a successful business of shoe stores located in Central and South America.

She had a beautiful home, and from the photos I had seen, a darling little girl. Enough money to have almost anything she wanted made her generous in offering me plane tickets to visit her but, since she was not aware of my real occupation, she couldn't understand how little time I had to visit.

I called Andrew from the airport as soon as I arrived. Rosa María wanted to meet me but I had told her I couldn't be sure which plane I would make.

Andrew and I worked up a plan. His cover would be a business man with an international company. He would stay in the Camino Real Hotel where I had a reservation. We would meet casually.

I had insisted on staying in a hotel, telling Rosa María I wanted to be able to sleep late, read, and catch up on writing – nothing out of the ordinary for a school teacher on vacation.

This being my first trip to Costa Rica, on the way to Rosa María's home, I played the tourist and found all I saw interesting and delightful. The abundance of brilliant flowers and fresh washed trees was similar to Mexico.

Lights were blazing from every window of the two story rambling house set back from the road behind a ten-foot-high fence. Acres of lawn surrounding the house were perfectly manicured. A call box was attached to the gate post. The cab driver got out of the cab and spoke my name into the box. Massive gates swung open allowing us to pass.

Rosa María was waiting on the front steps SO excited she was practically dancing. Beside her stood her handsome brother, Matt, whom I had not expected to see. Time flew away and I was back in college as I bounded out of the cab and into their arms. Rosa María and I were both laughing and crying. Matt held us both in his arms.

Dinner was a wonderful affair. I had convinced Rosa María to let Flor, her daughter, eat with us. Flor, so aptly named after the flowers, was a delightful, happy child. She sat beside me and held one of my hands through most of the meal. Rosa María smiled at the attention I gave Flor, knowing we had instantly bonded.

Matt was quiet but his blue eyes often found mine. Matt explained to me that he had flown down to keep Rosa María company while her husband was away on business. He added, "I wouldn't let her tell you I was here. I wanted to surprise you. However, I'm the one surprised. You, my little friend, have grown up."

I flirted and played with him but my heart wasn't in it. Maybe another time, another place, I could properly appreciate this warm, decent man who arrived at the wrong time in my life.

My bags were taken to the Camino Real hotel by the cab driver. Very late in the evening Matt drove me to the hotel. Promising to call when I was ready to be picked up the next day, I kissed him lightly on the lips and went into the building. My bags had been unpacked and my night gown lay across the end of the bed. It seemed like a year since Enrique had kissed me goodbye. Mexico seemed far away.

I slept soundly, no dreams to visit me. The big day came. Andrew flew in and we met "accidentally" in the dining room, at the breakfast brunch. He introduced himself as if he was a stranger. We couldn't play it too cool, the stakes were very high. In the early afternoon we had a casual poolside rendezvous and I filled him in on all I had deduced to date.

After I told him about the Acapulco incident he thought he would still have time to bust it.

"I'll fly out in the morning," he said.

My eyes suddenly teared at the thought of him leaving so soon.

He looked at me and knew there was much more I had not told him. Standing up, he spoke softly, "I'll come to your room at midnight and we'll talk."

Matt knocked at my door at 3.00pm. I was dressed in a white sun dress and sandals. Rosa María knew me better than Matt and my casual attire was part of my plan to convince her I had walked and shopped until I was so bushed I had a legitimate reason for leaving early to get a good night's sleep.

We had another wonderful visit. She had planned a quiet dinner, for the three of us, served on the terrace. Our conversations concerned our lives since college. I still kept to my cover as a school teacher. They had thought of me as one for years. Someday soon, I promised myself, I could be honest with them.

Back in my hotel room I changed into jeans and a tee shirt and settled down to wait for Andrew. Knowing the routine, I kept the lights off and unlocked the door at 11.45pm. At exactly midnight the door opened silently and he slipped inside.

I was sitting on the bed, wondering how honest I could be. He sat beside me and put his arm around my shoulders. This simple act of kindness from him opened the flood gates and I sobbed and talked and sobbed again. By now I was being held against his chest. He let me spill it all and never said a word.

I told him I had fallen in love with Enrique and didn't think I could turn him over to the agents.

After my sobs had quieted, Andrew said, "Enrique does not fit into my plans for you." He looked down into my eyes and took me with him as he lay full on the bed. His arms never released me. Holding me, he talked about the drug business and how it was ruining young lives. We reminisced about other assignments. Hours went by and we talked and he held me. Occasionally he kissed my forehead or my eyes.

Before dawn he said, "I need to go."

"No, no, please stay," I replied, "Keep me here in your arms, make me forget Enrique."

His arms tightened around me. "When I make love to you," he said, "It will not be to make you forget Enrique." Gently he put me from him and left as quietly as he had come.

The next morning in the dining room, as I stood before the buffet table, he walked up to me. In a low voice he said, "Hang in there and keep up the good work."

I saw him smiling and talking to other guests. Any observer would have assumed he was a business man looking for a little conversation because he was away from home and lonely.

The power of the United States government is awesome. Within hours after Andrew arrived in Acapulco, he had a ship, the USS Eisenhower, demonstrating off the coast of Acapulco, with navy seals in the water putting a beeper on the yacht with the Texas flag. That yacht was busted in the New Orleans harbor. It was registered to a Texas industrialist who said he had loaned it to his business manager – guess who took the fall.

8

IOWA

By the time I had spent another day in the company of Rosa María, Matt and little Flor, Matt had convinced me that I should fly back to Iowa with him the next day and visit for a few days. My head clicked into gear and I decided it wouldn't be a bad idea. Contact with Andrew would be easy and I wanted current information as to any bust before I returned to Ajijic. Three days wouldn't hurt one way or the other. I telephoned and left a message for Enrique that I was flying home for three days and left my parents' telephone number.

On the plane trip to Iowa, I realized what a good traveling companion Matt was. He seemed to sense that something was troubling me and left me to mull over whatever it was. A book consumed his attention except for a smile, now and again, aimed in my direction.

I decided it might be good for my psyche to feel carefree and not in love. Matt could accompany me to places where I could be a girl again and do all of those things I had not taken the time to do as a young woman.

I was sure I'd get lots of free advice from Clarissa. She would be delighted to see me. Clarissa was an uneducated black woman from the Virgin Islands. She had more soul and insight into people than any one of the more formally educated people I had met in my line of work.

Looking forward to seeing my parents was new for me but I found myself smiling at the memory of my mother speaking to father about six times to get an answer. He avoided many cocktail parties by pretending he hadn't heard her.

Once the plane had landed, Matt was no longer the quiet companion. We were home and it was time for us to say hello to the folks, his and mine, and to revisit all of the old places in my memory.

Even though Matt was a few years older than Rosa María and I, the favorite places were the same. We went to his home first. His parents were ecstatic to see us together. We were both from the same culture and social background. I could see wedding bells in his mother's eyes.

It crossed my mind also but only momentarily. At this point in my life, this small town life style seemed so peaceful. It's very hard to give up your training and discipline. I was feeling so ambiguous about what I must do to Enrique, if I continued on this assignment. I was probably vulnerable right now.

Matt had called everyone we had ever known or wanted to know. He arranged for all of us to meet at the Country Club for a buffet dinner and dance. He was so charming and sweet. I knew he was trying me on for size to see how I would fit back into this atmosphere and if I would enjoy being here again.

I didn't want to hurt him so I was friendly but distant. It would have been so easy. Our memories were so entwined, he was like a brother I friend, but more. He was the all-American hero type, very attractive, six feet three inches tall, blue sapphire eyes that hid nothing from you, broad shoulders, blonde hair and a smile that soon had you smiling with him.

I had been half in love with him since I was ten years old, and he was fifteen. He had betrayed me once and gotten married, but it didn't work out. If we had both remained in Council Bluffs, I might have been married to him with several blue eyed, beautiful sons and daughters.

I had developed another criterion, much more sophisticated and fast moving than my home town. Matt's dad had the state franchise for Coca Cola and Matt held an executive position in his company. They lived well but nothing like the scale I had become used to with Enrique. Comparison was not a good idea.

My mother and father seemed happy I was in town. Father was a little more absent minded than usual and mother was still trying to hide her alcohol problem. She had incorporated some new habits, drugs among them. Although the drugs were on a minor scale, she was taking barbiturates for sleeping and amphetamines for the bloating caused by all of her excesses. She was still beautiful as she always would be for me. The idea of Matt and I together was also gratifying for them, almost taken for granted.

As I was dressing for the banquet, Mom came into the room. I had been concealing most of my jewelry that Enrique had given me. After deciding to wear the pink slip dress I had worn in Acapulco, I was taking out the ruby ring, necklace, and earrings, wondering if they were a little up-town for Iowa.

Mother was speechless for a few minutes, then asked in a very motherly tone where I had gotten them. I told her a little about Enrique, not about the drugs. Saying that I had met him in Mexico, I eased into the fact that he was a wealthy Mexican man who owned a large pharmaceutical company.

"He's in a marriage of convenience and as divorce is practically unheard of in Mexico and the Catholic Church, he wants me to be his love and permanently reside with him in Mexico," I told her.

She got tight-mouthed right away and gave me her opinion of Mexicans. She thought I should return the jewelry, as it was far too expensive to be an acceptable gift. She continued by reminding me of Thomas Dye and how I had disgraced myself to the point of actually being sent away to college.

Thomas Dye. I hadn't thought of him in years. He was my first serious romance. He had come to Iowa State College from Puerto Rico. He was one of the best looking men I had ever seen: the product of a mixed marriage, a Swedish woman and a Puerto Rican man. His dusty looks were distinctive. He came upon the scene in my freshman year of college; it was instant "animal sex." We carried on a torrid affair for several months until I became pregnant and had to fess up to my parents.

They were indignant that I was pregnant and horrified when they met the father of their unborn grandchild. After a few weeks of tears and recriminations they convinced me I had no future unless I had an abortion. Before that came to pass, nature intervened and I miscarried. I was still not allowed to stay home for college, the gossip was too fresh. My new home was in Georgetown, Maryland with my aunt.

After recovering from the miscarriage, I enrolled in Georgetown University as a political science major. After that a friend of my father helped me to be accepted into the FBI Academy. I returned to being an excellent student, with no distractions from men, following my bitter experience with Thomas. The scandal of that affair kept me away from home but acquainted me with a good friend, my old auntie.

I blocked out my mother's voice and continued to dress, wanting Matt to be proud of me. I had every intention of enjoying the evening with my friends, who knew when, if ever, there would be another chance. Everyone was geared up for the party. Matt had the ability to control any situation. He would have made a good FBI agent.

We ate, drank and danced until nearly dawn. Afterwards, we piled in various cars to go to the "Golden Eagle", our old high school hang out. Matt had arranged for them to stay open for us. The night was made for memories. I knew before the night was over I would have to tell Matt that as much as I loved him, at this point in my life, I had other priorities that couldn't include him.

After Matt and I had our conversation, I knew it was time to fly away again. The following morning I ate a late breakfast with my father. From there I went to the library and called Andrew. I needed a shoulder to cry on. He was always there for me. After a tearful goodbye to my Mom, Dad and Clarissa, I was on a plane flying back into that mysterious double dealing political world of Washington D.C.

9

WASHINGTON D.C.

Andrew and I had decided that it was best if I stayed at my aunt's home. It would draw less attention this way and it would enable Andrew to be less observed.

My aunt was the widow of a famous, outspoken southern senator. She knew about Washington and its intrigue.

She had an older couple who "did for her", as she put it. They had been with her as long as I could remember and acted in almost every capacity. Extra help came in on a weekly basis and when she entertained. At the time I was living with her, I soon found out Dan and Sarah ran the household. Any time I needed something, they were there.

Betty, my aunt, was my only confidant in the family concerning my job. She wasn't too surprised when I told her about my work in Mexico. She knew how to camouflage a meeting. Calling Dan into the library, she informed him I would be staying a couple of days and we would have a guest for cocktails and dinner that night. Dan was given a menu, lobster bisque and the works, and keys to the wine cellar. She didn't need to tell him what corresponding wine. He knew more about wine than she did. Extra workers appeared magically, along with bouquets of fresh flowers.

I knew Andrew would enjoy the dinner and she would make the opportunity for us to be alone, which she did. After the superb dinner and an hour of repartee of Washington gossip, Andrew and I were in the library with a fire burning and a glass of Courvoisier in hand, the bottle on the table.

As soon as the door closed and we were alone, Andrew left his place by the fire and came over to my chair.

He bent down, taking my face in his hands. "Are you better?" he asked. "Do I need to fly away with you to the Yukon, or can we finish this assignment?"

He smiled down at me, and I replied, "I think I can last a while longer."

Sitting in the chair nearest me, Andrew told me he had erased me as an agent. He said no record of me as an agent existed anywhere other than in his safe deposit box. I must have looked shocked. It was as if he had read my mind. He went on to explain that when he had gotten an inquiry after the Acapulco trip, where I had met the governors of Texas and Arkansas, he knew it was time to erase me, so to speak.

I wasn't surprised that he was thinking of my welfare. He had always taken good care of me. Andrew and I had always had something special going. It was difficult to verbalize but if I had to, I would describe our relationship as a loving friendship with respect.

At the same time, I felt that if we ever admitted to ourselves we felt a sexual attraction, or acted upon those feelings, we would make the earth move, and our working world, as we knew it, would disappear. I guess the closest we had come was the time I almost got blown away in Greece and the second closest was recently in Costa Rica when he realized the danger I had gotten myself into.

Now it was necessary that I be honest again about my feelings for Enrique. I told Andrew I still had so much feeling for Enrique that I was in a real quandary. Enrique was so involved in drugs, and on such a high level, with so many prominent people, I couldn't come to terms with loving him and thinking about busting him at the same time.

Andrew turned serious and told me how important it was keep working on this assignment. He reminded me once again of the internal problems in the United States mostly caused by drug sales or use. He said it made our lives valid. We have to do something for the common good.

His only son had died of drug abuse. I had been aware of this for several years but he had never mentioned it. That night he told me about it.

His son was only fourteen years old. He was at a party with a group of kids experimenting with drugs. Someone had sold them coke which had been doctored with a poison. He took it first and became violently ill. He died several hours later in a hospital where his friends had dumped him in the parking lot.

Andrew told me his wife was very bitter and wanted him out of the DEA because they could not keep drugs off the street. His marriage deteriorated from his son's death and they were eventually divorced.

We spoke of how we Americans are into instant gratification. We aren't disciplined enough to wait for good things. He used the Chinese as an example of dynasties patiently waiting for their goals.

As always, he renewed my faith in self and country, and made me proud of the manner in which I served and was still serving. Too few people were left in America who were willing to sacrifice. By the time he was finished talking I was all gung-ho, out there and tote that barge, lift that bale. He was that good, he was sincere. That's how he became Bureau Chief.

I had spoken to Enrique several times since I had left Costa Rica. I had told him I was flying home to the United States with my friend. He had assumed my friend was Rosa María. I didn't dissuade him. Now I was ready to call him again to let him know I would be leaving for Ajijic.

Andrew and I had made tentative plans for communicating. Our communication would be sparse, only in emergencies, and when and if I got the date for when the next deal was coming down. Thank God we don't have precognition. If I had known exactly what lay ahead of me, I probably never would have left Aunt Betty's house.

I did leave it. The next morning I was up bright and early to fly off to New York and then to Guadalajara, Mexico. Just as I was leaving for Dulles Airport the phone rang. It was Enrique. He wanted to meet me in New York, saying we could spend a few days there, take in some Broadway plays, etc.

I knew Andrew would be interested in Enrique's sudden trip to New York. I acted anxious for the meeting, and in a way I was. It thrilled me to think of seeing him again but I was sure the trip was probably drug connected, and that I was only secondary. It served to enforce what Andrew had told me during our conversation in Aunt Betty's library.

I told Enrique I usually stayed at the Barbizon in New York and had reservations there. Hope springs eternal. Enrique had taken the presidential suite at Trump Plaza. He had a town house in the same building as Jackie Kennedy but his mother was in town on a shopping spree. I'm sure he thought I would succumb to his charms after so many days of being apart. It took a mighty effort to say no to canceling my reservations.

After he hung up, I called Andrew. He met me at the airport and I filled him in on the latest developments. I had hoped he would want to arrest Enrique in New York and it would all be over but he thought it was too soon. When they called my plane, Andrew took me in his arms and whispered in my ear, "Take care, my girl."

I was happy to see Enrique. It was like I had split my personality. One person was the young woman in love and wanting all of the entitlements of that love. The other person, mostly subdued, was a cold, calculating DEA agent ready to go to any lengths to catch him and his associates. At the same time, when he was speaking of love, I knew he was sincere because he didn't know that I was an agent.

I had played my role well when we last spoke on the phone. He had asked me if I needed money. He knew a school teacher didn't make a lot of money and I knew he must have been wondering about my travel expenses, maybe even a little suspicious. I told him my grandfather had left me a small trust fund that yielded a modest monthly stipend.

Laughing, I said, "It wouldn't even pay your florist bill." This little black lie would enable me to be a bit more mobile.

We did the usual New York junket. We ate at Regine's, The Four Seasons and several delis that Enrique knew well. We saw almost every play showing on Broadway. We talked often about our lives and what would have happened if we had met at an earlier time, before we had made commitments to others. I suppose Enrique would have brought me the City without my asking.

I remembered my mother having told me to return the jewels so, in a moment of consciousness, I told him I would allow him to buy me only one gift. He told me it would have to be something very special. One of our trips was to the top of the Empire State Building. That day he bought me a small gold charm.

"For remembrance," he said, as if I could ever forget him. I was right back under his spell, as if I had never been away. The same doubts about setting him up when the time came were back.

Although he acted the gay in-love swain, I could tell he wasn't only here to return to Mexico with me. My suspicion was confirmed on our third day there when he told me we were having lunch with some Arab clients of his.

The horror of the drug business was all brought back to me during that luncheon when I met the two men. They were documented major players in dealing heroin. They were thought to be responsible for seventy-five percent of the heroin brought into the United States. I could barely hide my disgust. Although the luncheon was very amiable and nothing was mentioned of drugs I knew that conversation would come later when they were alone with Enrique.

We were so "in tune" that Enrique sensed something was wrong. I played with my food and complained of a headache so we could get away from them. I was into my second persona—the DEA agent—ready to get whatever information I could from him.

Looking back, I find it hard to believe that I was able to act in a way that, to my knowledge, he never suspected me, not even once. I guess, because of my pretended illness, he thought it might be a good time to give me the one special gift he had mentioned.

We went back to my suite. He left, telling me to take a nap and he would pick me up later. He said we were going to have dinner with his mother at their townhouse. This really made me nervous, now I really had a headache. He didn't offer any explanations about how he had explained me to her. After all he was married. I thought it would be naive of me to ask.

A short time after he left, I had a phone call from the front desk saying a package had arrived for me and they were sending it up. When the bellhop had left, and I opened the package, I felt like a kept woman, a dope dealer's babe, and a wife, all rolled into one. There was a note telling me to "wear it tonight." It was a full-length sable coat, approximately four shades darker than my hair. It was stunning and included a matching hat and muff.

I thought my mother would have a heart attack if she could see this. I never once considered sending it back. It was one of the most beautiful things I had ever owned, even including all the jewelry he had given me. When he came for me, I was sure I was glowing as a reflection of his generosity and love. I was in my first persona, the "in love, in love with the world" mode.

On the way to the townhouse he spoke in a little more depth of his mother. From remembered conversations I thought "like father like son." My conclusion was that she also had had a loveless marriage. The endless shopping and trips to Europe were probably her form of escape during the marriage and had become her way of life.

I gathered from our conversation on the way over that he hadn't offered any explanation about me. I was with him and obviously meant a lot to him. She would either accept or reject me. I thought it was rather thoughtless on his part but he knew us both very well.

We had instant rapport, his mother and I, probably because of our mutual love for him. The townhouse was a penthouse, very European in flavor. She was exquisite and had rare taste. Although Enrique owned the townhouse, she told me she had decorated it for him and lived there more than he did. The collection of paintings alone was worth millions. She had a couple of old masters, a strong collection of the Matisse, Mary Cassatt period, several Picassos and Dufys.

I was remembering a previous assignment that had involved not only drugs but stolen art and forgeries on an international level. We had busted a ring of thieves in Madrid, but I had always felt the real culprits got away. I wondered if there were any stolen art or forgeries on these walls. We spoke of art for a while and in my persona as an inexperienced Iowa girl I played down what I knew, although I did say that I had taken an art appreciation course in college, just in case I gave myself away.

We passed a pleasant evening. The food she served was French in flavor and divine in taste. The servants were Mexican. Two served dinner and acted as wine stewards. There was also a butler.

Before dinner we had had drinks in the library served by a cute little *señorita* about twenty years old. If you counted the chauffeur, cook and cleaning women, it added up to quite a staff for one woman, another of the perks of the very rich. We said fond farewells with the usual, "I will perhaps see you again, maybe in Mexico."

As it was our last night together in New York we went one last time to listen to a few hours of Bobby Short. New York isn't New York without stopping in to see him. His romantic piano kept us in that benevolent state of love. We held hands and talked with the music in the background.

We were both nostalgic, he having just seen his mother and I having just came from visiting my parents. He told me several amusing anecdotes of his childhood and then asked about mine. I told him my father was a university professor.

Sharing with him about my mother was harder. I said that she had aspirations as a singer and actress in her youth. She had met my father before her career actually got started and had always felt she could have been successful. She had married well. My father was from an old New England family, conservatively rich and in excellent social standing. She was from Pennsylvania and also from a good family but had become the black sheep with her stage aspirations.

Her family forgave her after she married well. She never forgave them. She had become an alcoholic trying to prove herself to her family and his.

I explained that I was an only child and the only grandchild on both sides of the family. He wondered why I went into a teaching career. I told him I had always admired my father and was fascinated with children.

When we arrived back at my hotel there was a message from my aunt to call her. It was late and I said good night to Enrique and told him I would call my aunt early the next morning. I knew the message was from Andrew. I also knew that I couldn't call from the hotel that night.

Early in the morning I placed a call to my aunt, chatted for a few minutes and hung up. Then I got into my sweats and running shoes and left the hotel. After running ten blocks from the hotel, I felt it was safe to go into a phone booth.

Andrew had just gotten all the information on the big bust and felt I should let Enrique go alone to Mexico. I was to fly back to my Aunt. She was supposed to be ill but, in reality, would have a packet for me to review.

Andrew was leaving on business in another direction. I knew my aunt had already had the doctor pay a visit to make things look good. She was a stickler for details.

I saw Enrique off. We were both melancholy about being separated again. He left on a note of sadness with my promise that I would only be a couple of days behind him. My story had been that my aunt was ill and feeling very deserted. I told him since she was childless and had taken me in during college I owed her a little time.

The trip back to Washington went like clockwork. The packet Andrew had left for me gave me information that would help me when I was back in Mexico. He was very concerned about Hoffman. He felt that he was now completely loyal to the drug organization and would not hesitate to take me out if he suspected me in any way. Andrew's concern came through loud and clear and I had a premonition that Hoffman and I were locked in an inevitable life and death struggle.

Keeping my promise to Enrique, I flew back to Ajijic two days later. Andrew wanted me to bug Enrique's phone; I opted for bugging his car. I was sure by this time that he must do a sweep on his house. If he found the transmitter in the car he couldn't tell where it came from.

My house looked like a flower shop when I got back. I wasn't in the house five minutes before he showed up. The maid let him in and he walked through the house until he found me in my bedroom. We fell into each other's arms, telling each other how much we had missed being together.

It was late evening when I had gotten home. My faithful little maid had the place sparkling clean and had stayed to welcome me home. Enrique said he hadn't eaten, but didn't want to go out. He wanted to stay in with me and offered to have his cook come down and prepare us a meal. I told him that a meal had been prepared for me and I would be glad to share it with him.

I was so happy to see him, but I was quaking because of the bust. He didn't seem to have a clue as to my part in it. I guess by this time he was convinced I was who I said I was, with no hidden agenda. That sexual electricity we had, blinded him to everything. I couldn't let him blind me. I had seen just the tip of the iceberg on the drug scene. I was determined to help stop it, knowing my own personal happiness was at risk, if I even survived it.

The maid, Concha, let us know she was leaving and had fixed us a couple of drinks. We went into the den and settled on a couch to hold hands and look into each other's eyes. Enrique said he had been back two days and couldn't stand it here in the village where memories accosted him, even on his own terrace.

After a few drinks and much conversation, I got up to bring us the food prepared by Concha. Enrique followed me into the kitchen. "Don't leave me in there," he said, "You are not getting out of my sight."

Together we carried our light supper, chicken salad, crusty bread and white wine, back into the den and set it up before the fireplace. I threw some pillows on the floor and he sat down before the low table.

By the time I was seated beside him, there was a small jewelry box on my salad plate. He had bought me a gold witch holding a diamond in her hand like a crystal ball, another charm for my bracelet. He told me I had bewitched him, and that he never wanted to let me out of his presence again.

We sat up late, talking about our trips and making tentative plans for our future. I was deliberately being evasive although I knew I would be with him until I had a situation in which he could be busted. My other reason for being evasive was I really didn't want to be committed to him or want a commitment from him.

I knew the chemistry between us was getting to be a problem for us both. Something held me back. My gut feeling was that once we became that familiar it would be all over for me, I would lose control. He told me he had a condo in Puerto Vallarta and had to go there on business. "Please come with me," he said. "We can fly down and spend a few days in the sun."

My only contact was there so, of course, I needed to go with him. If he only knew I never wanted to be away from him again. I was madly in love. I decided there and then that on this trip we would become more than just friends. I think he was coming to some decision also. I didn't know it then but he had decided to be honest with me. I also think he knew of my decision to succumb to him physically. I guess we were both setting the stage in our minds for the great seduction scene. I know I was really nervous.

We had a couple of days before the planned trip to Puerto Vallarta. I think Enrique wanted to seem part of the social scene so he wouldn't look suspicious or stand out in the village. He asked me to meet him at the Posada the next day for drinks and dinner.

Mexican peasants have a naive curiosity about strangers. They will ask you anything, even something very personal. I once had El Pequeño ask me how much money I had. I told him I had enough to buy his horse, making a joke out of it. Then we got into where would I keep the horse, even if I should buy it. He laughed and said he would get the money and the horse. They are easily distracted. I was afraid of these Mexican type questions from the Posada crowd.

The usual group was there and they saw us as a welcome diversion. I believe I told Liz I had been to Costa Rica to visit a college friend. I hoped they didn't know Enrique and I had both arrived back from the same destination. He didn't mention it to them and neither did I.

They were all ready to fill us in on the latest scandal. Two lesbian "Mari Macha" types had arrived in Ajijic and had been thrown in jail over night for brawling in a local cantina. They were all abuzz with this, so Enrique and I were no longer the most current item. We got into a conversation about homosexuality, until the gay priest and his love showed up.

We then switched to traveling and Liz spoke of going to Greece in a few weeks. I got back into my DEA persona and became very closed mouth. I mentioned immediately that I had only traveled once abroad. The year my father took a sabbatical and we went to Spain. That year I had been fifteen years old. Those comments got everyone to talking about their various experiences while traveling.

Enrique and I finished our drinks and went into the dining room before it closed. That group of boozers would forget about eating.

After dinner he asked me if my embargo was still on regarding receiving more gifts. I smiled as he pulled out this small jewelry box. It was a tiny gold Chinese junk with magnificent detail. The word junk was the key word. I couldn't help myself, I remembered those terrible heroin dealers we had lunch with in New York.

I thanked him properly for the gift but said I thought it was time for me to go home. Always so sensitive, he thought I might not have liked the gift. I assured him I did, but that the traveling had left me tired. We walked to my house and after a long good night kiss, he left singing as he walked up the beech.

I was exhausted; this being a dual personality was getting too intense. I have been involved before on assignments but never an affaire de coeur. I was becoming like an alcoholic, looking at it one day at a time. I was making my decisions on a daily basis, not the long term ones I had been used to.

I walked through the house and admired my flowers, which always soothed me. That's something I had really gotten into in Mexico: fresh flowers on a daily basis, sometimes even from my own yard. That didn't happen often because Enrique kept me well supplied. In this beautiful little village during the rainy season they have Indians outside the markets selling orchids. Can you imagine buying a natural spray of several orchids for two dollars? They grow wild in the mountains.

After a sleepless night I got up early and went looking for El Pequeño. I needed to get on Vesuvio and ride until I was worn out. El Pequeño met me on the way there and told me he had heard I was back and just knew I would want to go horseback riding. The insight that Mexicans have is incredible. My theory is they haven't filled their minds with trivia. They hear it and forget it. Their criteria are less developed because they have had less exposure.

We decided he would pick up the horse around twelve at my house. I went riding off with a lightness of heart after speaking with him. The beautiful tender blue sky with its softness of clouds, the lake and kelly-green mountains helped me forgive myself.

Enrique didn't show that morning. He was busy arranging our trip to Puerto Vallarta.

10

YELAPA

Our time flying down had been spent on lovers' talk, nothing on a business level. We landed and were met by a limo and whisked away to the condo. Puerto Vallarta is beautiful, with tropical vegetation. The condo was right on the beach and decorated in excellent taste. Of course, by this time I didn't expect otherwise.

My suite was filled with flowers and several packages. He had done it again. There were several beach outfits and colorful dresses made by my favorite Mexican designers, Galion. Two small jewelry boxes were on the stand by the bed. One of them contained a bracelet of pearls, with matching ring and earrings. The other contained a little gold yacht for my now famous charm bracelet. I never went without it.

We got our suitcases unpacked, with the assistance of his household help, and settled in. As soon as that was accomplished he wanted me to go with him to the yacht basin where he had another yacht called the Elena. This was a business trip for him and he appeared anxious to take care of it.

As far as I could tell from the meeting on the yacht, he was orchestrating another drug shipment. I met his crew; among them was Hoffman, the rogue agent. There was no mistake, Enrique was the jefe again; everyone deferred to him.

He had told me that he wanted to take me to the Island of Yelapa, about forty-five minutes by boat from Vallarta. As they were preparing the yacht for the short trip, I noticed that Hoffman seemed nervous that I was aboard. I was on deck and Hoffman passed me several times. He seemed to hesitate as if he wanted to ask me something.

As we took off, he took the opportunity to ask if I spoke Spanish. I said, "Very little."

Then he asked where I was from and how I had met Enrique. I ignored his questions and asked where he was from and how long he had worked for Enrique. I was sure Enrique had filled him in on me, but he couldn't be sure what I knew about him. He knew that any discrepancy casually mentioned to Enrique could get him killed.

What he didn't know was that I had memorized the pertinent things in his dossier I had back in Washington. The dossier described him as a man forty-two years old, graduate of the top ten percentile from the FBI Academy. He was five feet ten inches tall, Greek heritage, spoke several languages like a professional, and looked and sounded today like a well-educated Mexican.

He had been responsible for several large busts, one in the Fott Worth area. He had worked on it for several years and netted the arrest of several big time nationwide dealers. Those years he worked undercover on the Fort Worth bust, Andrew had trusted him completely.

He had worked for Enrique about two years. The fact that he seemed more affluent than warranted by his salary and bonuses, and his reluctance to turn in big names, led Andrew to think he may have been wrong in trusting him so completely.

I knew Enrique had come to depend on him immensely and he should have been coming up with some hard facts. Andrew had told me that he turned in a few minor dealers, but the investment in time was not paying off for the agency.

After Hoffman left me, I walked around the deck looking at the other boats. As I passed an open porthole I could hear Enrique and Hoffman talking in the galley. Hoffman was telling Enrique that if I was going to be with him I should be aware of the risks. Then Hoffman came down pretty hard on Enrique, telling him how foolish it was to be involved with someone, just when they were pulling off a fairly big deal, something that would net them both millions.

Enrique countered with, "It's still my operation and I make my own decisions. This isn't just any girl. I'm in love with her and I fully intend to be completely honest."

Even though they were speaking in Spanish and didn't know I could understand them, I didn't want to risk listening further so I strolled on around the deck to the other side.

From the moment Enrique and I had stepped on the yacht I knew Hoffman had busted me. I could see recognition in his eyes. What he didn't know was Andrew and I had already busted him. I was sure he would make the opportunity to speak to me. He couldn't go to Enrique about me without involving himself. I was shaken by the conversation and knew that I would have to find my opportunity with Hoffman.

Enrique was the typical macho Mexican. He could sense something was going on with me and Hoffman. In his mind it was sexual. Because of the sexual connotation, and maybe because Hoffman had defended my right to know the truth, I would find it difficult to be alone with him. I was sure he was also looking for the opportunity to speak to me again.

Yelapa was a really primitive island, much more so than I had imagined. Enrique wanted to take me to a boutique located on the island belonging to a friend of his. In fact, his friend had grown up in Ajijic. Her family had been one of the first foreigners in the village. She was known for her beauty and hospitality. She had been married to a famous movie director, divorced and settled on this little piece of land.

As we were walking to her place someone came up to speak to Enrique and evidently needed him to go somewhere. I could see he didn't want to leave me with Hoffman, but he couldn't leave me alone on the beach.

"I have to be gone for about thirty minutes," he said, "Hoffman, take her to the boutique."

The minute Enrique walked off, Hoffman started to tell me that he knew who I was. He said he had seen my picture on Andrew's desk during my time I was working in Greece. He said he had waited in Andrew's office one afternoon and Andrew did not show so he left.

He had actually met me one time. He described a scene in a Washington restaurant. He said he stopped by to say hello to Andrew as we were dining. His name was different then, he had been wearing a beard.

I vaguely remembered, but that wasn't his point. He let me know in certain terms that he was not going to be busted, that it would be him or me.

Both of us knew that our lives would be snuffed if Enrique knew anything. I could only dissemble at this point and pray that he believed me. I told him that I had fallen in love with Enrique and there was no way I could turn him in.

"Since I can't go back to my life, neither can you. Why don't we both forget we ever heard of the DEA and stay in Mexico? I'm not averse to living with money, and evidently you must have learned to like it a lot."

We walked on toward the boutique and he never really committed himself to my plan. He only smiled and said, "Welcome aboard."

I was feeling really threatened and not sure he believed what I proposed. I knew I had to get rid of him before he found an opportunity to make me have an accident. There was no reason for him to take a chance on me. I hoped that his chauvinism led him to believe I was sincere.

When I had started in this spy business my aunt had given me an antique poison ring which had belonged to one of our relatives who had it made and used it during the civil war. Andrew had given me a fatal drug to put in the ring in case I was ever in a situation that required one. I knew now was the time to use it. I would bide my time.

We were arriving at the boutique and our time was taken up by introductions to Rita. Shortly after, Enrique was back and smiling. I gathered that at one time he and Rita had a thing going and she still carried the flame. She couldn't keep her hands off him. It was a good diversion for me.

I was jealous but had more important things on my mind. I had never actually plotted someone's murder. I felt like I was caught in the middle of a murder mystery novel. This time I had to be the bad guy. It wouldn't be easy.

We had lunch at Rita's and I limited myself to one margarita while the others had many many more. I kept my eyes and ears open. Observing Hoffman wasn't difficult, but it worried me that he had Miguel in a corner deep in conversation and I couldn't hear a word they said. Miguel and I had a good rapport but one word from Hoffman and I knew I'd be history.

They poured themselves back on the yacht just at sunset and I pretended to be as tipsy as the rest. We watched the sun set and excused ourselves to take a short nap before dinner. There was no sleep for me but I did try to rest and keep my mind clear. The only thought I allowed myself was that it had to be done and soon.

Possessing a calmness I dared not question, I dressed with great care, wearing a pale blue silk cocktail dress and my Wedgewood antique poison ring. Hoffman soon joined us for pre-dinner drinks. That's when I made my move. It was fairly simple. On a yacht everyone is almost always looking at the sea or the sky. I dropped the poison in his Scotch glass, excused myself and went below to the head.

When I returned a few minutes later, Hoffman was gone and there was a strange silence from Enrique and the crew. I asked where Hoffman was and they said he had gone below, that he wasn't feeling well. I never saw Hoffman again. I was sure that Enrique had him tossed overboard. His business wouldn't warrant a death or subsequent investigation.

11

PUERTO VALLARTA

I had been in many dangerous situations on various assignments but had never had to kill. It left me more sure than ever that I had to get out of this business. I claimed to be slightly seasick and hung over as we docked back in Puerto Vallarta.

Enrique was very subdued and suggested that I go back to the condo and he would see me shortly, I arrived back at the condo with my constant companion, Miguel.

I wanted so much to reach Andrew, but it would be impossible at this time. Although I was sure that some of the other agents would notice Hoffman's absence, none of them would know what had happened to him until I could explain to Andrew.

When I was finally alone, I went into the bathroom and vomited. I ran water in the shower to cover the sounds. The tile was cold on my cheek when I stretched out and lay there on my stomach.

Later I crept to bed. I must have fallen asleep. I awoke to Enrique entering the bedroom looking distant and distraught. I was hoping he didn't think I had anything to do with Hoffman's death, that he would attribute it to fast living and drug abuse. He sat on the bed and took my hand.

"I don't think you realize how much I love you", he told me softly.

Then he proceeded to tell me that he hadn't been completely honest with me. I recalled the overheard conversation between him and Hoffman. He went on to say that he loved me and wanted to marry me, but because of finances and religion he could not divorce his wife. I would be recognized as his second wife in public but first and only in his heart.

Then he explained that, although he had many legitimate businesses, the majority of his wealth came from an illegitimate one: cocaine dealing on a very large scale. As if I didn't know! I was in agony to have him trust me to the point of confiding. He said he wanted out but couldn't get out at this point. I knew that feeling well. I was so tempted to bare my soul in return but it would be instant death without time for explanations. There wasn't a doubt in my mind that he was a brave bold warrior and we were engaged in a war. He was used to making hard instant decisions.

The trip wasn't going the way I had planned. I had been all ready for the big seduction scene. Once I had made up my mind to let it happen, I was anxious for us to be lovers.

He started talking again. He told me he was here to set up one of his biggest deals yet.

I kept telling him I didn't want details. I guess it was like confession for him since it had been so long since he had someone he thought he could trust completely.

He went on to tell me about Hoffman. He said Hoffman had been his number one man, but he liked to shake up his organization every year or so. Now his brother-in-law, Luis Fonseca, would be elevated to that post and Hoffman had a new assignment.

His mind seemed to skip from one thought to another. He was back telling me that he wanted me by his side, every minute of every hour of every day. It was what I wanted also for as long as possible. I asked about the risk factor to me.

Again, he assured me I would be protected at all times. There are no words to tell you how cherished and loved I felt as he explained the grandiose plan he had developed to shield me.

Enrique told me our next trip would be on the Lear jet and that we were flying to the Caymans. We would be meeting, casually of course, some of the same people we had partied with in Acapulco. Everyone, Enrique included, would be putting large sums of money in the numbered bank accounts in the Caymans but they were also there to pull down the biggest coke deal ever. A tanker, of Turkish registry, was on its way to the Grand Caymans with twenty tons of coke and uncut heroin with a street value of billions of dollars.

My mind was going ninety miles a minute. I couldn't think of the magnitude of what was coming down. I had to think of how I could get back to Andrew. Enrique still appeared let down, depressed. I wondered if he regretted the impulse to tell me everything. I assumed we would be flying out of Vallarta. Sometime between then and now I must at all risks make a telephone call.

In the meantime, I needed to assure Enrique that everything was fine. I suggested that we go out for a quiet dinner and maybe some dancing. He wanted to stay in.

Well, I thought, now or never. I told him to make himself comfortable and I went into the big walk-in closet and took down my sexiest clothes. I dressed before a big long mirror and then returned to the bedroom where Enrique was stretched out on the bed.

I sat down and started being aggressive with him. He was amused and amazed. I had always let him be the aggressor. It was all a real effort for me because I couldn't overcome the fact that I had literally murdered someone.

We were heating each other up with looks, touch and feel. I had always stopped at a certain point and could see that he thought I would do so again. No way was I going to stop this night, I owed myself one.

I told Enrique about taking a modern dance class in college and about learning how to belly dance. I suggested that I dance for him. I had packed my costume thinking it would be a way to initiate my seduction scene. Now I thought it would be a way to amuse and excite him and bring him out of his depression. A belly dance usually lasts approximately eight to ten minutes. Mine may have lasted five.

He was pretty excited from the moment I came out in my costume of fine blue silk. My body was very visible through the thin layers of skirts. I thought it a very original way for our first time. It made me feel good and excited me as well. Although I hadn't danced in a long time, the performance was effective.

When I was close enough, Enrique reached up and pulled me on to the bed on top of him. We ripped each other's clothes off like savages. His lips stayed on mine. In a few minutes our true feelings came through and we slowed down, kissing and caressing each other.

We were both moved by the depth of our feelings and lay there, in each other's arms, without words, until we started again by mutual consent. There we were, enjoying excitement, sensuality and love, the "whole enchilada." We made love until the wee hours of the morning and I fell asleep in Enrique's arms, exhausted.

I awoke to a bright tropical sunshine and Enrique walking into the room. I had not felt him move or leave. He was loaded down with a breakfast tray of flowers, orange juice, my favorite breakfast—*chilaquiles*— and yet another jewelry box. What more could one as for?

In the state I was in, one could only speak in superlatives. The jewelry box contained a tennis bracelet consisting of one and a half carat diamonds of brilliant clarity. He told me he had bought it the second day he met me, to give to me at our moment of becoming lovers. This was so beautiful and tender it brought on hugs and kisses and back to bed.

It was already past noon and the phone had rung several times. He knew he had to answer it because of what he was setting up. I never wanted to leave the condo. I knew what I must do eventually. He didn't want to leave either. He suggested that he get dressed and go to the yacht to give orders and come back for me, giving me a chance to take a leisurely bath and time to dress without being rushed. Then we would have a late lunch and leave for the Caymans.

When he left, I agonized a little while about using the phone to call Andrew. I couldn't leave the condo. I was sure the bodyguard was right outside the door. When Enrique was telling me about his dealing he had mentioned sweeping his houses, yachts and telephones periodically. I was reasonably sure his phone wasn't bugged. My logic and need got the better of me and I called Andrew. I told him to go somewhere and call me back.

In Washington everything is bugged. He used a pay phone and called me. I told him what was coming down. He was incredulous. I told him about having killed Hoffman and why. I reported that Enrique had promoted Luis Fonseca, his brother in law as his new chief. He said he would check up there to see if anything had leaked concerning the big shipment and Hoff-man's death. We tried to make plans for phone contact but finally decided the calls would have to be random at best.

Enrique came back about two hours later with yet another jewel case. He told me he wanted to give it to me over lunch, but couldn't wait. It was a five carat emerald of the finest, clear-est green, with four large diamonds on each side. He said the color and clarity of the emerald was the color of my eyes as we were making love last night. Who couldn't live with someone who talked like this?

Our late lunch was soon over and we wound our way back to the condo to do some light packing so we could board the Lear jet. All depression had left Enrique. He was challenged by the logistics of what would be the biggest drug deal ever and he had found the love of his life. It was his first time to be in love and to be completely honest with the person whom he loved.

I knew it all, the exhilaration he felt and his love for me. I also knew that through my deceit I would take all of those feelings away. He would probably never trust again.

12

CAYMAN ISLANDS

I wasn't playing a role when I told him I loved him. However, a very difficult role emerged as we wound our way over the Sea of Cortez, Gulf of Mexico and into the Caribbean. My agent role settled firmly on me as I remembered Andrew's words. I told Enrique that I wanted no part of the deal.

He discussed it openly with me, and agreed he didn't want me on the yacht when the deal came down. We decided I would stay at the Radisson Hotel and he would see me as much as he could.

I had obtained enough information, even while protesting I wanted no knowledge, to know we would be in the Caymans two days before the deal went down. I was really curious as to why we had arrived early. Enrique went to my suite with me. He waited, looking out over the bay, as I changed into a cool aquamarine skirt and matching blouse.

Together we went into the elevator and then onto the terrace outside the dining room. A waiter escorted us to a table. The terrace was covered with green awning with golden fringe. Bright pots contained orange, red and yellow flowers. The sun blazed in a clear blue sky. I had very little on under my cotton skirt and blouse. It felt good outside, so thinly dressed.

While we were eating a lunch of calamari and salad with tall glasses of iced tea, my favorite bodyguard arrived at our table. Miguel told Enrique, in Spanish, that a helicopter had arrived for him.

Sending the messenger away, Enrique reached across the table and took my hands. He told me he had to leave me for the night. He was flying to Puerto Rico on business.

Picking up the briefcase he had carried all morning, he said, "Let me walk you upstairs. I need a kiss before I go."

I had looked out a window in my suite earlier and noticed a helicopter pad on the roof of the building next to the hotel. As soon as Enrique departed, I opened the terrace doors and stepped outside on the balcony. I was six floors up. My objective was to wave to Enrique. After only a few minutes, I could see men getting into the helicopter. The blades were already turning.

To my shock and horror, as the helicopter lifted up it flew close enough that I could easily identify the United States Presidential Seal on its door.

Enrique didn't see me, he was looking the other way. Breaking out in a cold sweat, I blindly made my way back inside and bolted the door. I slid to the floor, sitting with my knees against my chest. Tears were silently sliding down my cheeks.

The bodyguard was protecting me from outside my door. The telephone operator was a stranger I dare not trust. My mind screamed for Andrew. No voice answered me.

I knew now why Andrew had erased me from the files, but others in the San Francisco office knew of me. Would enquiries go any further if I was not listed anywhere on the computers?

There was only Andrew to share my heavy burden, and I couldn't reach him. It was just too dangerous, not only for me but for him.

Dawn found me lying on the bed, weeping and scared. I knew Enrique would return in only a few hours. I struggled to the bathroom and filled the tub with cold water.

Forcing myself to lie down in the tub until the water covered me, I realized the next hours would probably determine my future credibility with Enrique. As politically involved as this deal was, I would be dead if he or anyone close to him realized how upset I was.

The water treatment revived me, to a certain extent, but I knew I needed more. I rubbed myself dry on a thirsty white towel and got into my pink sweats. Opening the door surprised Miguel.

I smiled sweetly and said, "I need a run. With Enrique gone, that room gets smaller and smaller."

Although he seemed surprised that I was up so early, he didn't indicate that he was concerned. I'm sure he wasn't looking forward to running the beach with me, but maybe he was bored and didn't mind. At least he was pleasant.

At the steps of our hotel, I started out in a slow trot. Miguel was right beside me. The beach was just a few hundred yards in front of us. I find it much easier to run on wet sand. From the beach I watched the surf as I ran.

Miguel and I spoke a few words to each other at first, but we were soon into the routine and couldn't waste breath on conversation. The long stretch of beach eventually curved into a cove. By the time we reached it Miguel was lagging behind me. I dropped down onto the sand.

When Miguel sank beside me he commented, "You amaze me. How did you get in such good shape?"

"Running away from the boys," I joked back.

After we rested a few minutes I asked Miguel if he was married. He answered that he was and told me his wife's name was

Selina. He was proud as he boasted, "I have four sons. They are strong and take care of their mother when I'm away."

"You look too young to have four sons," I told him.

He was flattered at that remark and also by my interest in his family. We ran back, the breeze blowing in our faces. At the steps of the hotel I asked Miguel if I could buy him a cup of coffee in the coffee shop.

He declined saying, "Thank you *señorita*, you are one kind lady but Enrique would not like it." Walking across the hotel lobby Miguel said to me, "*Señorita*, I want you to be very careful. Life is not the same in a foreign country as it is for you in America."

I smiled at him and told him I was grateful for his concern. At the time I thought it an innocent warning to a woman he had learned to respect. We went up in the elevator and I thanked him for going with me. Inside the door, I leaned against it. Act One was over. I felt better after the exercise and a good performance. I gathered my courage and telephoned Andrew.

13

BETRAYAL

The telephone call from Natalie from the Cayman Islands, her last day there, stunned me into immediate action. The fact that a helicopter with the presidential seal had picked up Enrique put me on guard. This would have to be played by ear and very discreetly.

I spent many hours at my desk going over and over again the list of people I could trust. They would have to be people who had power and integrity enough to risk their political careers for the good of the nation.

During all of this mental debate there was my underlying concern for Natalie. After all of these hours I had come up with a scant nine people and a loosely devised plan as to how we would handle this explosive situation.

Our surveillance, thanks to Natalie, had several top level politicians involved at a national and state level. What this would do to the United States Government and its credibility was insurmountable.

This would have to be played as close to the chest as possible and hopefully without a leak. Because of the credibility factor it had to be top secret and only known to a selected few. These eight men and one woman I had chosen had never, to my knowledge, been involved in any sort of governmental scandal, or anywhere near one.

I took my list and left my office. There was no way I would risk using my office phone or my home phone for the plan I had in mind. I needed help and guidance and these nine outstanding intelligent people could help me if anyone could.

I drove over to Natalie's aunt's home. She ordered drinks and acted as if my showing up in the middle of a work day was a normal procedure. We talked of pleasant things and finally she asked me if I'd like to see her garden. Little old ladies often do that. As soon as we were out of range of any ears she asked what she could do for me.

I told her I needed to have a top secret meeting of nine very important people and myself and that absolutely no one could know about the meeting. She was intrigued and flattered that I asked. I knew she was the sole of discretion. I made the telephone calls from her library with her practically standing guard outside the door. I asked each person to leave their office and call me back using an unlisted phone number Aunt Betty had not given up after the Senator's death.

It took me the greater part of the day to arrange the meeting. They all agreed to come to Aunt Betty's home. They were told to come at 8.00pm as if they were attending a dinner. There would be no dinner, we did not have the time, and I knew Aunt Betty would have the house cleared of servants except the couple who had been there for years. They were used to important people coming and going. They would be excused for the evening and could go out or stay upstairs in their apartment as usual. Nothing would seem out of the ordinary.

Included in the select nine, were the Vice President, Secretary of State, Secretary of Defense, Director of the FBI, Director of the CIA, Director of the Department of Justice, Ambassador to Mexico, Speaker of the House of Representatives and Speaker of the Senate. It takes powerful, dedicated people to carry out a task such as had been handed to us.

My plea was strong and convincing. Natalie had given me irrefutable evidence. I could see that each one was stunned at the magnitude of what lay before us. They too saw what would happen to the fabric of our country if there should be the slightest leak before the actual operation. The country could not afford a leak, even after it was over.

The government people involved in the drug dealing would have to be handled very discretely but firmly. It was too explosive for the country to even consider punishing them with imprisonment, but they must be made to understand that they had no choice but to resign from whatever office they held and could never again hold a position in any city, county, state or national government. They must be required to return all monies and property that could be traced to actual drug dealing. This would be very difficult, considering the risk of a leak if we pushed too hard.

The group seemed to feel that some of those suspects might be willing to cooperate in disclosing all persons involved from the lowest level street dealer to the highest. The plan we were developing had started out simple but as we progressed it became more complicated. What do you do with an ex- president who is a master criminal? We all knew from our investigations before the election that he had communist ties in his youth and had participated in anti-American demonstrations.

The decision was not mine. People with more power than I, and even greater responsibility, made the final commitment to arrange the assassination of the President. That assignment was given to the Director of the CIA. The group wanted it done about a week after he would resign due to ill health. It was too dangerous to have an ex-president who could, at any time, decide to sell our country's secrets to a foreign power for money and revenge.

The rest of the plans concerned actually picking up the drugs to keep them off the streets of America. We had a location on the Turkish freighter. The secretary of the navy would deploy a U.S. ship off the coast of Grand Cayman; this would look like an ordinary maneuver and wouldn't raise the suspicion of anyone. Then the navy seals aboard would go in and bug the freighter. We would also have a submarine in the vicinity ready if we needed it.

My understanding from Natalie was that there would be a boat leaving the freighter at various times, making contact with designated ships and unloading, coming back, reloading until all the merchandise was unloaded. Each newly loaded ship would take off for its own particular destination. We knew once each individual ship was loaded they would have no further contact with the other ships. This left us a clear field to confiscate each ship individually with just a small risk of any of the others being aware. Their clandestine operation worked to our advantage.

We made a body count of the people involved. Among them we had the governor of Texas, the governor of Arkansas, a prominent senator from Florida, and one from New Orleans, and the President. Among the list were also a few minor government officials. The question uppermost in all of our minds was how did it get so big? Was this the first time as a group? I definitely had egg on my face. My buddies in the CIA and FBI were in a state of shock. Had this been going on for several years and none of us had picked up on it?

We all knew it had to stop here. We knew if we failed it would bring shame to all of America and we were determined not to let this happen. Little did I know when I sent Natalie to check on the double-dealing Hoffman and a suspected drug lord what a can of worms I had opened.

Because of Natalie, we had not arrested Enrique Vázquez. In point of fact he did not have possession of any drugs, he only had money in the billions of dollars. He would go back to Ajijic, thinking he was safe but, once we got Natalie out, he too would be arrested.

Our big chore, after the completion of the confiscation of the drugs, would be to face the President and the other politicians involved and convince them to resign quietly. We all felt this needed to be handled simultaneously. There were ten people in our group, including myself. We would go in teams of two and visit the top five suspects.

The Secretary of State and the Director of the Justice Department were assigned to talk to the President. I would give the signal when the drugs were all in our possession. At that time the visits would be made. The vice president had taken charge of our group, so some of the stress I had felt was lifted to his shoulders. I was impressed with the way he assumed all of the responsibility. He seemed to grow before our eyes into presidential stature.

14

AJIJIC

Enrique and I were back in Ajijic, my *casa chica* practically abandoned. I remember the day so clearly. I wasn't an agent at my best, I was a woman. His house was surprisingly quiet. People were usually milling around wanting his attention for the phone, visitors and so forth. That day only maids and gardeners worked gracefully.

We sat on the east terrace, facing the lake. The water in the lake was a rippling blue. Breezes that slide across the waves carried the scent of jasmine.

My dress was the vivid red Enrique loved; he had tucked a red hibiscus behind my ear. He wore black trousers with a black silk shirt, open at the neck. I had survived the Caymans. We had been home one day. I had told Enrique that although I loved him I didn't know if I could stay.

"The drug business is bad, and it bothers me. You have children and a wife. How can we make a complete life separate from them? Maybe it would be better if we tried to just remain friends," I solemnly said.

His black eyes matching his attire were serious and unsmiling as he repeated his declaration of unending love. He made me believe he couldn't see his life without me. He informed me again his marriage to Raquel was not important. He still maintained he couldn't divorce her but he said it didn't matter. He said he wanted babies with me.

His voice was so soft I could hardly hear him as he told me, "Red hair, and your big green eyes on my own little girl would make me a king."

Breakfast was served to us but we ate very little.

"I don't want to leave your side," he declared.

My eyes teared. "Please understand," I answered, "your life-style is so foreign to me." My chest ached with the pain of my love. I wanted to shout the truth: that his life was in danger. I knew if I did I would be dead. Instead I sobbed quietly, "I guess I need to talk with my father."

Enrique whispered, "It makes me love you all the more to see your respect for your father. In Mexico, the father is always to be respected."

Toward evening, we were both exhausted from a day of emotional conversation. Social activities planned were canceled, by mutual consent.

"Come, *mi amor,*" he said, taking my hand and leading me through the house, up the stairs into his bedroom. I had started to cry again and he softly told me, "We will work it out."

The smoldering passion we had felt, but held at bay, all day, sparked into a roaring fire between us. Just inside the door his hands found my hips and I so soft I clung to his chest. It seemed the most natural thing in the world to hold each other. The thought of my love was terrifying. He was so wonderful, how could his deeds be so horrible?

My tears trickled down my cheeks, wetting my clothes. Sleep was a long time coming. The loving was over, so was the assignment.

The next morning, I felt him kissing my hair before I opened my eyes. His big smile told me, in his mind, he had our problems solved, our lives planned. He handed me a small black box and waited for my reaction as I lifted the lid and stared at the very large yellow diamond displayed inside.

"It's your engagement ring," he stated. "The other part of your present is this," he said, holding up two airline tickets. "I want you to go talk to your father. It's also important that I talk with him. I intend for you to be my wife in all ways, and I must make him see that. You need his consent to be happy. You and I will want them to visit us here. I will tell him that I can afford you and that you will share everything I have," he said with strong voice.

Then the voice changed, "Do you think they will accept me?" he whispered like a little boy.

"How can you get away, you are always so in demand?" I asked.

He smiled, "A weekend is all we need for me to meet your parents, we won't even tell anyone where we're going."

Three hectic days later, I was sitting on one of the iron benches in the plaza. Enrique had been working and planning frantically, making phone calls, canceling meetings and giving assignments to cover any emergency during his absence. He expected to be out of touch all weekend and that made some people in his organization very nervous. Today, he had been in Guadalajara since early morning and I didn't expect him back for three or four hours.

I was left pretty much on my own to pack my things. Enrique had told me to pack what I wanted for the trip and he would have everything else moved into his house while we were gone.

I had enjoyed the tranquility of the plaza for an hour. Little brown skin children played around me, laughing at everything and nothing. It made me wish I really was a teacher. I had walked to the plaza at twilight with the intention of placing a telephone call to Andrew. It seemed to me a pretty safe hour to go about unobserved.

The telephone I intended to use was in a small business, advertised on a sign as *"Larga distancia."* I could see into the building from my vantage point on the bench. A group of five people had been standing around inside, one of them talking on the phone. Finally the people left all together. Mexican families do things together and I guess that family was making an important call. I bolted across the street before my courage left me, praying for a few minutes of privacy.

Small Mexican businesses are often located in the front room of a family home. The remaining rooms, usually located behind and above the business, are still maintained as a home.

I walked in and, finding myself alone, placed my call using perfect Spanish. What I had not realized was that the owners of the business were relatives of Miguel, and that he was visiting them in the next room. I had my back to the open door separating the rooms; I was facing the street to observe anyone coming in and also to muffle my voice.

Miguel placed his hand on the receiver and removed it from my hand. He hung it back in the cradle, holding my arm.

"Let's walk to the plaza, *señorita*," he said.

My heart was in my throat. Fear caused me to stumble and I would have fallen on the cobblestones if he had not supported me. We walked through the plaza to the darkness of the trees beyond before he spoke again.

"I like you *señorita*, but you are a dead woman. Enrique will never allow you to get out of Mexico."

My mind was wild, searching for a plan, an escape.

"Please Miguel," I stammered, "Do not jump to conclusions."

"I know about Hoffman," he answered. "Hoffman told me he had reason to suspect you and that if anything happened to him, to watch my back. I haven't told Enrique. I wanted Hoffman to be wrong. Now I must go to Enrique to save myself and my family. They would have no qualms about killing my wife and sons."

"Can you give me some time?" I asked in a small voice, tears starting down my cheeks. "I really love Enrique and I don't want it to be this way."

Miguel stared at me with a dark sober look. I know he believed me. He called me by my name for the first and last time, "Natalie, I will wait one hour, God go with you."

Walking as fast as I could without drawing attention to myself, I hurried back to my house. Inside I quickly put my cowboy belt around my waist inside my skirt. The belt contained $5,000 in US dollars hidden in an inside zipper. Next I grabbed the pillow case which hid the jewels Enrique had given me. I threw my walking shoes inside the pillow case on top of the jewels. Taking a jacket from the closet, I ran out the door. Food and all other essentials were far from my mind.

I knew I had to trust someone and my instinct was that it should be El Pequeño. I ran east on the beach until I was in his back yard. I could hear him talking to the horses as he fed them. His voice was calm and soothing.

Hearing my footsteps, he turned to me and listened as I blurted out, "I'm in very serious trouble. I'll pay you to help me escape. Please let me explain on the way."

"What can I do?" he asked.

"Saddle the horses and get me a pair of your pants. I think we'll need to go over the mountains. Hurry, I only have a few minutes, fifteen at the most," I answered.

El Pequeño quietly saddled the horses. I stood in the shadows cast by the house. He was swift. After the horses were saddled he went into the house, returning about five minutes later with a backpack on, carrying a couple of Mexican blankets which he tied onto the back of the saddle.

I had slipped into my jacket, not because I was cold. It was one thing less in my hands.

El Pequeño brought the horses into the shadows, tying my pillow case in back of my saddle as I mounted Vesuvio. Not knowing the path we would take, I fell in behind him, as he rode Cinco de Mayo out the gate. We did not speak further.

He rode east but stayed away from the beach. On one of the last streets of the village, he turned north and we rode the horses at a brisk walk to the base of the mountain.

I glanced back for the first time. Fear had kept me looking forward as if the peril would overtake me if I did not. I could see lights all over the village. My watch told me we had a bare half-hour head start, if we were lucky.

El Pequeño was risking his life for me and maybe for a promise of money. I wondered what explanation he had given his wife. I hoped I could ask these questions later but at that moment my only purpose was to put at least one mountain between me and my pursuers.

15

ENRIQUE

I could see my reflection in the mirror on the wall behind my desk. My eyes were a stunned angry black. They had often had that look before she came.

Miguel was gone. I told him he had done a good job and he could go home to Monterey. A hacienda with a large farm to work with his sons was his dream. It would come true. I would buy it for him and give him a monthly income.

He had earned it. He was a good friend. We played together as boys. If I didn't get him out of my sight, I knew someday, in a rage, I would kill him. He had brought me the news that my love had been betrayed. How could I ever look at him again?

I remembered the first drug deal with the Colombian when he offed my Miami contact. I still regretted that. It was the first time I was involved with the violence of murder.

Could Natalie have actually killed Hoffman? Directing my men to take his body to the house of my uncle, I had waited on the yacht for word of the cause of death. Someone had poisoned him. I knew then, an enemy had been aboard my boat. Natalie never entered my mind. We had made love for the first time that night. Remembering, I wondered, "How could this be?"

The airport, train depot and bus station were under surveillance. A small army of men had quickly been assembled. The orders were to bring her to me.

I knew I should have ordered them to shoot her on sight, but I couldn't. I had brought her in. I would have to be the one to take care of it.

Three hours had passed since Miguel's phone call to me at my office in Guadalajara. The helicopter brought me home in minutes. Until I arrived and she was nowhere to be found, it wouldn't register. My nerves were exploding; I couldn't sit still any longer.

Luis came into the room as I stood up.

"I'm walking to the Posada to see some people. If I get any clues I'll follow them up. Tell Manuel to keep behind and to stay outside when I'm in a building. If anything turns up, send someone for me. Remember the instructions, don't hurt her," I finished.

It was a bright night, stars and a big moon lit the streets and the water. I had walked with her, holding hands, down this beach, to the plaza, just last night. It was all so unreal now.

"Where is she?" I wondered.

The Posada was crowded. Walking up to the bar I ordered a whiskey and turned to glance at the room. Several people I knew casually from Liz Bryne's party were sitting at two big tables shoved together in the corner. Liz wasn't with them. Maybe Natalie was with Liz at her house. I knew my next stop.

Whiskey in hand, I wandered casually over to the group and said my hellos. After a reasonable time of casual conversation, I asked if anyone had seen Natalie around. Nancy said she had seen her earlier sitting on a bench in the plaza. I knew the bus ran down that street, she could have been waiting for a bus.

Fighting the need to ask if she had luggage, I excused myself and went back to the bar. Taking a few minutes to ask the bartender if he had seen Natalie, I tipped him and left. Nothing much so far. The bus station was covered so I turned my steps to Liz's house, two blocks away. Manuel kept faithfully behind me.

The doorway was set back and wrought iron gates were located on the street. I rang the bell and waited. A young girl of about thirteen came to the door. She made no move to open the gates. I asked if Liz was at home.

"She is not so good, *señor*, and is resting," she replied.

I told her Liz's friend, Natalie, was supposed to visit and asked if she had arrived.

"*No, señor*," she answered.

I thanked her and turned away. Motioning for Manuel, I met him at the corner and told him to stay behind and watch the house. Liz might really be sick but it sounded pretty convenient to me.

Finishing my instructions to Manuel I started walking back toward my house. Suddenly, a thought came to me. Natalie had another good friend I had forgotten, a friend with horses.

Deciding to be a better investigator this time, I walked to the house of El Pequeño but went to the back gate facing the beach. I meant to check to see if the horse I had seen Natalie ride was inside.

El Pequeño was in the yard and saw me come inside the gate. Calling out, "*¡Buenas noches!*" he walked over to me.

I could see both of his horses inside an open shed which he evidently used as a stable.

"What can I do for you, *señor*?" he asked.

"I may want to rent a horse tomorrow for a few hours, would you have one available?" I asked.

"Only Cinco de Mayo," he replied. "*Señorita* Natalie has first choice with Vesuvio. She plans to ride tomorrow."

I told him I'd let him know if I needed Cinco de Mayo. He was calm but once the idea of the horses had entered my head, I couldn't let it go. It was one way she could have disappeared so quickly.

If nothing happened soon, I'd send some riders up the mountains and some into Jocotepec, a village ten miles or so away. She could ride there easily; she was good, even though I had teased her otherwise.

She was also very intelligent, and she knew her life was in danger. She would not be easy to catch.

Hours had passed and we were now scouring for a boat that might have been hired to row across the lake. Manuel had watched Liz's house for three hours with no sign of anything to question her illness and no presence of a guest revealed.

Natalie must feel the presence of the hunters like a wounded animal, I thought, before rage returned, and I pictured her dragged, screaming before me.

Most of the village slept. Sitting on my terrace so I could watch the moonlight on the lake, I could hear music from the Posada. The scene I had left yesterday evening was probably the same. The double table of drinkers were no doubt still drinking and telling themselves how much fun it was. I wanted the music to stop, people to go home and leave me to grieve.

Natalie's eyes always teared easily. Mine did now for the first time since my father died. I missed my father, I realized, after all this time. If he is somewhere where he can help me, I wish he would, was my thought.

The phone sounded shrill in the night. It was 1.45am and a *gringa* had been spotted on a train to Mexico City. She had red hair and had a *rebozo* over it as if to disguise her appearance. None of my men in Mexico City would know her. I had two choices, I could send someone from here who knew her or I could fly up and check it out for myself. It sounded like such a good lead, I decided to go.

Ten minutes later the helicopter was in the air. We followed the path of the train for an hour before we spotted the long black shape with a beaming head light. We flew ahead of the train to see if there was a town that seemed feasible for a train stop. We spotted Querétaro and anticipated the train's arrival there to be in about half an hour.

We landed the helicopter, causing quite a stir, and I walked to the train depot with two men to assist me. Money convinced the station master to keep the train long enough for us to search out the *gringa*.

Forty minutes later the train puffed into the station. Expecting to pick up mail and passengers and move out again, the engineer was surprised to see us board the train, two from the front, and me from the end. We left the station manager to explain. The passengers were sleepy and it was time consuming, making sure we saw every face.

There were only ten cars to check. I had searched three when my assistants arrived at the far end of the fourth car. It had to be the one. My heart pounded as I spotted red hair ahead of me. The *rebozo* had slipped in her sleep and the girl was oblivious to my need. I turned her face toward me, and beheld a stranger.

At dawn I was back on the terrace trying to out-think Natalie. A different kind of respect for her gripped me. She was a worthy adversary. I had enjoyed living on the edge. It gave life a zing, besides being profitable. Evidently my girl Natalie had also lived on the edge.

For the moment, I was convinced she loved me. It wasn't too different to being involved in a war. She was a spy and must be found, but did she have to die? I had been trying, since the girl on the train, to convince myself that I could save her. I had not slept and not eaten. I knew I must. My strength was important if I was to win, but what did it mean to win?

What little energy I had left was suddenly gone. I went inside to try to sleep for an hour. Does she sleep? I wondered. I have my bed, but where does she feel safe enough to close her

16

ANDREW

Andrew wasn't in his office when Natalie's call came through. An anxious secretary reported to him that an aborted call was made.

"Bring me the tape," he ordered.

Her voice sounded clear and calm but the message was short and unfinished. "This is Natalie. It's urgent that I speak with Andrew."

The secretary replied that he was not in.

"Tell him I'll ...," and Natalie's voice ended with a click, as if someone had hung up the phone.

Could someone have come into the room where she was making the call, and then she hung up? The alternative was more frightening. Had someone heard her make the call and she was not able to hang it up? Andrew's secretary, Ronnie, short for Rhonda, had reached him in the field. She knew his dread of aborted telephone calls.

With no more clue than her voice, no return call, he knew he had better get the ball rolling. A computer on his desk told him the agent located closest to her, Tom Mcintyre, was in Guadalajara, if he could reach him. It was midnight in Guadalajara; hopefully he would be in bed.

The phone rang four times before it was answered. "Hello," a sleepy gruff voice responded.

"Tom?" Andrew asked.

"What the hell do you want? I just got to sleep," Tom mumbled. "Natalie may be in trouble, lakeside," Andrew told him.

He explained the telephone call and the fact that several hours had passed without another call. Tom was awake now. A fellow officer in trouble was a call never ignored. After a brief conversation with Andrew in which he received a few facts and several instructions, he was dressed and out the door.

Tom had been stationed in Guadalajara for three years. He knew the Lake Chapala area well. He also knew it was very unlikely that he would be able to find any news before morning, but he would hit a few bars just in case.

The Posada was his third stop, and to this point he had learned nothing. Business was still booming inside. He had been in the Posada and remembered the large room which housed the bar. Wood was scarce in this area but it was used lavishly in this building. Many years of polishing had left a satin sheen that glowed in the soft tight.

He remembered on one trip that someone had pointed out a water mark on the wall about three feet above the floor. The lake had risen that high during an extra heavy rainy season and the place had flooded.

Tom walked to the bar and ordered a beer. With the beer in hand, he slowly made his way around the room.

"What's happening around the village tonight, any action?" he asked several times.

The boredom of the customers told him a lot. Their purpose for the evening was to get drunk. Most had succeeded. In the corner, where two tables had been shoved together, he learned a little more. Getting desperate he told this group that he had just gotten in town and was looking for a friend.

"Has anyone seen Natalie tonight?" he asked.

A woman of about sixty tried to give him a sexy smile as she replied, "Enrique was in earlier looking for her so you'll have to settle for me." The group all laughed as if she had said something hilarious.

Tom stayed and joked a minute or two and excused himself. He went back to the bar and ordered another beer. When the bartender left to serve some drinks he poured it on a potted plant and wandered outside as if he had nothing to do.

The walk up the beach from the Posada to Natalie's house was a couple of blocks long. As he neared the vicinity of her house he spotted two men, one partially hidden by the large columns on the front porch. The other man was next door watching her house from the roof.

As Tom got closer he staggered a little and began to sing in Spanish. By the time the men spotted him, he was near the water and must have appeared to be a drunk. Taking his time, Torn threw some rocks in the water, sat down a while on the sand and finally sauntered on up the beach.

There had been no lights in Natalie's house. It was pretty evident someone had a welcoming committee waiting for her.

His car was parked at the Posada. Caution made him approach it from the far side of the building. He unlocked it and got inside.

As he drove away, a Mexican man came out from under the wharf, which was located almost in front of the Posada and started jogging toward Enrique's house. Enrique would be interested to know someone else was looking for Natalie.

Andrew was in his office waiting for Tom's call. He grabbed the phone on the first ring.

"Yes," was all he said.

Tom explained all that had happened. They both knew that Natalie was on the run.

"A plane leaves here at 6.10am for Guadalajara," Andrew said, "I'll be on it. Meet me at the baggage terminal."

Neither had a plan but they both agreed they had better come up with one. Andrew sat at his desk with his head in his hands. Why had he sent her? Sure she was good, but the law of averages can eventually get anyone. She had to be ok. After this he would make her quit. Maybe he would quit too. He had to find her before Enrique did. He had secretly pictured them growing old together too many times to let some drug lord put an end to the brightest light in his life.

Tom met the plane and felt better seeing Andrew walking toward him.

With no preliminaries Andrew said, "We will set up a command post in your house and get in touch with every agent in Mexico. Since we don't know where she is, alerting other agents, but leaving them where they are, may be our best bet. If one of them can spot her we are in business. You and I can take turns with the phones and listening locally and lakeside for information."

Tom smiled, he was feeling better. Andrew was in charge and by damn they would find her.

Andrew wanted to get as close to Natalie's trail as he could and decided the best way was to be very visible. He breezed in to Ajijic and drove right up to her house. He could see the men who were observing the house. He parked the car and walked through the front gate.

As he reached the porch, one of the men stepped from behind a column and asked Andrew if he could help him. Andrew introduced himself as Matt Halstrom. He said he was a friend of Natalie's and asked if she were home.

"No," the man replied, "She is not at home. I'm not sure when she will return; maybe you would like to talk to her fiancé, Enrique Vázquez."

Enrique's office was down a hallway from the front entrance. Following a servant down that hall Andrew felt as if he had been here before. Natalie's descriptions of the house and its layout were professionally accurate. A door opened and he was admitted into the office.

Enrique sat behind a massive rosewood desk. The furnishings were rich and comfortable. Enrique stood and offered his hand across the desk. Andrew smiled and offered his in return.

"My name is Matt Halstrom," he said. "I am a friend of Natalie's, from her home town. She was recently visiting my sister. I saw her in Costa Rica and promised if my trip took me to Mexico, I'd stop by."

Enrique had sat back down and was studying Andrew. "I'm glad you came by to meet me. Natalie never told me about a good looking brother in the picture," he commented.

After a brief pause Enrique spoke again. "She left for a couple of days. She's with a girlfriend on my yacht somewhere off Puerto Vallarta."

"Just my luck," replied Andrew.

Enrique then became the perfect host. He rang for a servant and asked that drinks be served on the terrace.

"What do you drink?" he asked.

"A Cuba Libre is good; if not, anything will do," Andrew answered.

Enrique came around the desk. "Good," he said. "Let's go outside, it's so pleasant today."

They walked through the house and observers would have thought them friends. Andrew was a couple of inches taller. They were about the same age. They both appeared relaxed and enjoying each other's company.

Once they were seated on the terrace with drinks in front of them, Enrique asked, "What do you do in Iowa?"

"My father and I have the coke franchise for the state. We work together," answered Andrew.

"My father and I worked together in pharmaceuticals until his death a few years ago," added Enrique.

Andrew was surprised at the ease with which they spoke. He knew Enrique must be searching for Natalie and was very likely to suspect the coincidence of a visit from an old friend. Enrique never gave anything away.

Andrew had to admire the guy's guts. His organization could fall around his ears, with him in prison and you'd think he didn't have a care in the world.

After they finished their drinks, Andrew asked some questions about Guadalajara and then said he thought he had better take off.

"If Natalie has stood me up," he said, "I better get back to my job." Enrique stood to walk him out, saying, "I'm sure we'll meet again. When my girl comes home I'll tell her she missed you."

The two enemies had met and taken each other's measure. Neither would underestimate the other in the future.

17

THE MOUNTAIN

At last we were on our way. I was thanking God that El Pequeño knew the way. The mountain was covered with thick foliage. I didn't think Enrique would think of me going into the mountains but he was smart and he knew I could ride. It would be a long and dangerous journey, especially at night. El Pequeño figured we would be at least four hours compared to one and a half hours in daylight. He felt once I we got to Los Cedros he could find me a way out.

I needed to get word to Andrew as soon as possible but there was no use to think about it now. I wasn't ready to tell El Pequeño that I was a DEA agent. I let him believe Enrique had suspected I was having an affair with Miguel and had threatened my life. That it was imperative he not find me.

As we were going over the mountains, El Pequeño wanted to talk. It seemed the feeling of danger had opened a flood of memories for him. He didn't doubt if Enrique found us he would kill us both. He seemed to be feeling very protective of me and was man enough to do what had to be done to protect me.

His memories were of the many times he had gone with his father to pick up and smuggle pre-Columbian treasures. The danger was always there, if not from smugglers like themselves, then from the authorities, mostly judicial police. He said they always had buyers for these treasures. In fact they had a preferred clientele and went as far away as Guerrero for pieces from different periods. Most of the clients were Americans interspersed with some Europeans, mostly German. The family had been pretty successful at this and was able to buy small pieces of land and several horses.

His Dad had died the past year of alcoholism. His mother had opened a *fonda* on the highway selling *menudo* and *pozole* to the early morning crowd, made up mostly of the town drunks. He said he seldom smuggled anymore, he preferred his life free of fear of prison.

He loved his horses and cultivated his land. He belonged to the *charros*, a group of men who have trained horses they use for celebration days in Mexico, of which there are many. He's telling me all this as we pick our way over the trail. I'm listening and interested but I felt so threatened by all that has gone down.

Had Miguel yet told Enrique? What exactly did Hoffman have time to tell Miguel? How much had Miguel overheard when I was trying to call Andrew? He couldn't have heard much because the phone call was certainly cut short but he did hear me place the call in perfect Spanish when I supposedly did not speak the language. My mind was darting in and out of possible scenarios. I hoped I was able to give proper responses to El Pequeño.

As we went into a valley to climb up the second mountain, El Pequeño asked if I would like to rest. I was tired but we had only been traveling about forty five minutes to an hour and I was too afraid someone might be on our trail. The trail was getting steep and we were riding single file when my horse, Cinco de Mayo, stepped on shale rock and went into a slide. El Pequeño grabbed for us but not before my horse's fore foot had gone under him and I was thrown off.

I rolled down the side of the trail and was stopped by a mesquite bush. El Pequeño pulled Cinco de Mayo up and then came down after me. I was scratched up but nothing broke. The horse had sprained a fore hoof, which forbade him from being ridden any further.

We talked it over and El Pequeño felt the only solution was for him to return and get another horse. I could either chance it and go with him or stay and wait on the mountain. I was afraid of the mountains alone at night, but for me going back was much more dangerous. I elected to wait.

We had passed a small cave about a half mile back and we walked back to it. El Pequeño helped me to check out the cave and he gathered some mesquite wood to build a small fire in front of it to keep out any predators. We both felt the fire could be a danger but the lesser of the two.

He took the saddle and blanket off Cinco de Mayo. It would be less of a burden for the horse and he could make better time coming back. He gave me one of his serapes and his machete, said he would be back as soon as possible, and left me to spend one of the most torturous nights of my life. As a DEA agent I had worked under some very primitive conditions but never alone in a wilderness like this.

He was no sooner out of my sight than I became aware of the sounds and silence of the mountain. There were the hoots of several owls that seemed to be speaking to each other from a long distance. One would hoot and then several minutes later it would be answered.

This was somewhat like the joke about being in a hotel and hearing a shoe drop in the room above you. In the morning after a sleepless night waiting for the other shoe to drop you find out the man in the above room has only one leg. The mind goes into strange spaces when one is under stress.

I soon forgot about the owls, squeaky rodents, etc. I had a more serious problem. The fire had attracted several large coyotes, or maybe the cave had been their lair. I thought I might die on this mountain, but not without a fight. I was so grateful to El Pequeño for providing me with the things I would need to keep them away.

I kept telling myself, "Don't be afraid." I had a pile of wood, a pile of stones to throw at them, and the machete in case one should rush me. They were howling and circling, but I would never know if they might have attacked.

A sheep herder, from down in the valley, had been attracted by the fire and he thought he might find some good company. His arrival frightened the coyotes away, but now I had another problem. He was surprised to see a *gringa* this far up in the mountains and of course was curious as to why I was there.

I mentioned El Pequeño right away because I was sure he would know him. I explained about the horse and why I had been left behind. He was a low minded person and immediately thought it was a romantic tryst. I had to let him believe that for I had no other rationale.

Unfortunately it led him to believe that he was more macho than El Pequeño and could give me a better time. I was thinking he may be worse than the coyotes. I had kept the conversation going in a light hearted way and he kept bringing it back around to sex, what he could do for me, and all that stuff.

I had the machete by my side hidden under the serape. I hoped my black belt in karate would not come into play. At any rate, about the time I think he would have made a move, we could hear El Pequeño whistling to let me know he was back. The sheepherder stayed and shared some tequila with us and excused himself and went on his way.

When the sheepherder had gone, El Pequeño told me that right after he had reached his house and put the horses in the stalls, Enrique had come into the back yard very quietly before he saw him. He said Enrique asked if he might have a horse available the next day and had told Enrique that Cinco de Mayo would be available but Natalie had planned to ride, and she would be using Vesuvio. He said Enrique said he would let him know if he needed the horse. I didn't need to wonder; now I knew Enrique was turning over every stone.

By this time it was the early morning hours. El Pequeño brought food, coffee, water and another blanket. He suggested we sleep for a while and then head out to Los Cedros. He said he thought of my predicament and had a plan we would discuss when we awoke. We each rolled ourselves into serapes and fell into a restless sleep.

El Pequeño had good common sense and a natural intelligence. Upon awaking he told me he felt Enrique would continue to look for me. He said he thought betrayal through sex was a very powerful driving force for a Mexican man. He wanted to know if I had actually deceived Enrique.

I seriously considered telling him the truth at this point, but couldn't bring myself to do so. I simply told him things are not always as they seem, and swore there was nothing but friendship between myself and Miguel.

We packed up the horses again and rode the rest of the way down the mountain and across the valley to the next one. As we rode, El Pequeño told me his plan for when we got to Los Cedros. He had a *tia* (aunt) there who was a widow. He thought she and I could dress as if we were in mourning and take the second class bus out of there into Guadalajara. She would travel with me all the way to the border.

It would take some planning but it could be done. The idea of going to the bus station in Guadalajara scared me to death. I knew Enrique's men were crawling all over the place by now. El Pequeño told me not to worry: by the time they finished with me, I would never be recognized.

He had brought his horse, Reyes, for me to ride. She was a little mare, a little slower than Cinco de Mayo but better trained for the mountains. I sure wasn't ready for a repeat of the previous night.

We waited on the outskirts of the village until it was dark and people were pretty much settled in their homes. In these little Mexican villages people usually go to bed soon after it gets dark. His relatives lived in an old dilapidated hacienda. It had a fence around it built in the shape of a quadrangle.

Entering from the wrought iron gate the first thing you saw was the church, or chapel as they called it, long in disuse. The quadrangle was probably about three acres of land with houses built along the walls. I found out later it was built in the late fifteen hundreds and had belonged to some distant relative.

It was situated a little way out from the village. I'm sure not everyone living there had the same last name as El Pequeño but he had a host of relatives there that resembled him, so much so that it appeared they had all been cloned.

We were welcomed into his *tía's* home. I don't know the exact explanation given for me, it was done out of my presence, but I seemed to be accepted. Doña Chuy bustled around making us food and *té de azahar*, which is supposed to have properties to make you sleep. I didn't feel I needed it as my body was telling me I had been awake for an eon. Doña Chuy was a woman in her early fifties. She had been widowed for about twelve years and her youngest child, a daughter, lived at home.

I still hadn't given away my ability to speak Spanish. In this way I would know if I was in danger, without their knowing I had comprehended.

His *tía* and her daughter, who was named Yolanda, went on cheerily chirping about trying to make me comfortable while El Pequeño tended to the horses in the stable. It was decided I would share Yolanda's bed and El Pequeño could sleep on the floor curled up in his serape. They showed me to the bed and I fell into it. I was almost immediately asleep listening to the murmur of Doña Chuy and El Pequeño making plans for my escape on the morrow.

18
DOÑA CHUY

I awakened in the early morning hours and lay there, thinking of Enrique and my betrayal of him. Doña Chuy started stirring around, and I decided I'd better get up. I tried to keep in mind the circumstances that had bought me to this situation, and tried to remain as unemotional as I could. I dressed and went into the kitchen where Doña Chuy was preparing *desayuno* (breakfast).

El Pequeño gave me a run down on the plans they had made to get me out of there. The last bus came through the village at nine o'clock at night and we would be on that bus.

We spent the day dying my hair black and using the bark of some tree that had properties to dye your skin. I soaked my body, face and hands in this dye several times during the day. By nightfall I had beautiful golden skin, the color of light cinnamon, along with the black hair. In widow's weeds, and with my new coloring, my own mother wouldn't have known me.

I would be accompanied by Doña Chuy and Yolanda as far as Guadalajara, where we would buy tickets to Torreón. From Guadalajara I would be accompanied only by Doña Chuy. I would play the role of a grieving widow, crying and saying the rosary. Doña Chuy would accompany me as if my family feared for my mind. She would be wearing black also.

They didn't have a schedule for the buses out of Guadalajara. We didn't know if we would be stranded there for several hours. That part of the plan made me plenty nervous. As it turned out, we were there for about two hours.

My patience was almost gone from sitting and acting my part as the widow. Yolanda headed back to Los Cedros with a mountain of instructions from Doña Chuy. I thought about my parting from El Pequeño. How fond I had gotten of him. I felt I had a true friend in him. I was crying when I left him, and if he hadn't been a macho Mexican he would have been crying also. He didn't want to accept the five hundred dollars I pressed into his hand, but I insisted.

Would I ever see him again? I doubted it. As we were waiting for the bus I saw several of Enrique's men come in the station and start looking around. The men looked at us, one of them, long and hard. I let the *rebozo* slip to show my black hair, bent my head and fingered the rosary with my eyes closed. Doña Chuy gave him such a look he was intimidated and walked away.

At last, we were on the bus, without further incident, headed toward Torreón. About three hours out of Guadalajara the bus was pulled over and searched. I pretended ignorance of what was happening, and Doña Chuy told me it was the immigration people looking for an American.

Could this have been Andrew? After Miguel had hung the phone up so abruptly, Andrew must have listened to the tape of the call and was probably very upset and wondering what had happened to me. Maybe it was Enrique's men. The long arm of drug dealing could reach anywhere, as I had found out. It could have been just a routine check, but I doubted this. I knew if it had been Andrew's people, he would have found some way to signal me as to the reason for the search.

Then I really got upset and wondered, how did they know which bus to check? Were they checking all of them? If so, this would take a small army. My mind got off on a tangent and I almost lost control. This was a luxury I couldn't afford in my situation. I soon calmed down. It helped having someone by my side. If I lost control I would be risking Doña Chuy's life as well as mine own. I wouldn't allow myself to do this.

We were stopped and searched several more times, by these and sometimes different people, on our trip to Torreón. By this time, I was sure it was Enrique's task force.

Our plans had been, if we were not threatened or investigated in any way, that Doña Chuy would leave me in Torreón and return to Los Cedros. If threatened, our alternative plan was to go to a Casa de Huespedes; these are guest houses where travelers of reduced circumstances sometimes stay in their travels. They are primitive in nature, usually with the bathroom shared by everyone in the guest house. We agreed this was what we should do after all the bus searches.

Upon arriving in Torreón, we caught a local bus to the center of town. I wasn't ready to risk a taxi. After questioning a few of the locals we soon found a Casa de Huespedes and Doña Chuy signed us in. I was still supposedly the prostrate widow lady.

By this time we had been some twelve hours on the bus, and both of us were tired and weary. We were lucky. Because I was in deep mourning they had given us the only room that had its own bathroom. We fell on the bed and lay there for about half an hour without talking. Doña Chuy finally spoke and asked if she should go get us something to eat. I was certainly in agreement with this suggestion and while she was gone I took a long hot bath.

Relaxing in the tub gave me an opportunity to think about my next move. It was urgent that I get in touch with Andrew.

I had to think of how to do this without jeopardizing Doña Chuy, Andrew or myself.

As I lay soaking in the tub, I couldn't keep my thoughts from going back to my time spent with Enrique. I remembered the bubble bath we had taken together the morning after our first night of love making in Puerto Vallarta. As I touched myself lightly noticing the red public hair against my brown skin, I wondered if he would have liked me as a *morena*. I would never know. I thought, now is not the time for memories, it's the time for saving your skin.

That little phrase clicked into place the memory of a friend of mine whose family had a ranch near Villa Ahumada, a little village close to Chihuahua. Why hadn't I thought of this place sooner? I remembered the time I had gone with her to the ranch. She had had an abortion. It was an Easter vacation. We were in college. She knew her family would be at the beach. They thought she was spending her vacation with me at home. We had gone, instead, to the ranch for her recovery from the abortion.

I wondered if by chance she could be there. Her skin was saved by the abortion. Her family would have immediately disowned her had they known. Getting out of the tub, I thought I would discuss the possibility of Doña Chuy and I going there.

The ranch had been inherited by Dolores' father from his father. It had been in the family for years, an old hacienda type ranch of about two thousand acres. At the time I was there, they raised sheep and had apple groves. It was located at the foot of the Sierra Madre Mountains. Oil had been discovered on the ranch and there had been some big dispute during the time of Lázaro Cárdenas. I knew some of the ranch land had been confiscated.

I was sure someone would be there, that I knew, and that remembered me.

The ranch had been primitive in the way you got there, by bus or car, but it did have its own landing strip. Dolores and I had gone by car. The ranch house itself, because it was a family home, was pretty luxurious then, having all of the accompaniments of elegant living. I remembered a thermal spring among the apple trees, riding horses, and large cozy bedrooms. Yes, I decided, if Doña Chuy agreed, this would be my next stop.

Doña Chuy was in agreement. She arrived back to our room just as I was putting the finishing touches on my eyes. Now that I had access to a mirror I kept glancing into it, trying to come to terms with yet another identity.

Doña Chuy, always resourceful, had brought back some of my favorite food: *carnitas*, tortillas, avocado, flan and a soft drink. *Carnitas* is one of Mexico's favorite dishes. It is cubes of pork cooked in its own juice, crispy on the outside and juicy inside. With tortillas, avocado and hot sauce it makes a fabulous taco. We ate as if we were war orphans and hadn't eaten in days. There was no time for niceties, we were starved. After literally porking it up for about ten minutes, we found time to talk.

I told her about my friend's family ranch and asked her opinion. She thought it might be an answer to her prayers. She suggested we call the ranch but I didn't even know if they had a phone. They hadn't had one when I was there. I rejected the idea anyway, for the element of surprise. We only had to figure out the logistics of getting there, in the most convenient way, and the most secretive.

She decided we should stay in the room overnight. She went in to take a bath. I had to decide how I would, or could, arrive at the ranch in disguise.

Maybe we could get the second class bus to Las Delicias, the nearest town to Villa Ahumada, spend the day in a Casa de

Huespedes there, get rid of all or part of my disguise, then late
at night get a taxi and go on to Villa Ahumada.

I could send Doña Chuy to Chihuahua and she could get a plane
back to Guadalajara. We talked long into the night about our plans.

She indulged her curiosity and told me she was sure that my
running was something more than being caught "in flagrante." I
was tempted once again to tell the truth but there was nothing
to be gained by it, and my life to lose.

The next day we were up to catch the first second class bus
coming through the village heading for Las Delicias. Doña Chuy
had taken some money and gone around to the shops buying
up a few decent clothes, mostly *fayuca*, so I wouldn't appear as
a fugitive when I arrived at the ranch.

She had also purchased some mineral oil and chemicals to
get rid of my brown skin. We decided to leave my hair black.
It would be too difficult to get it back to its natural color and
one can always explain away the impulses we have to do something different with our hair. It would also serve to keep me less
noticeable. I was feeling somewhat secure that we had gotten
away, and had calmed down a little, thinking I was almost home.

As we boarded the bus to Las Delicias, Doña Chuy was
strangely silent and introspective. I wondered what she was
thinking of this whole episode and of me. She had told me
that she suspected more than it appeared. I was thinking how
it would be a story to tell her grandchildren. I knew she seldom
crossed the mountain to Ajijic, so I was safe for a while. El
Pequeño had sworn her to secrecy.

My mind went back to my college years as the bus motored
toward Las Delicias. I thought how fate takes strange turns. I
had been sent to Georgetown away from home because of an
unwelcome pregnancy and had met Dolores. She had the same

problem. It was our commiserating that had eventually led me to this bus trip and back into her life.

We had been good friends before and during her short pregnancy, but the guilt of my knowing about her abortion had left a constraint between us. Although we remained friends, speaking sometimes on the phone, exchanging birthday cards, and the occasional letter, we were never as close. We had seen each other at college reunions so I wouldn't be walking into a cold situation.

I must think of some reason for showing up there. Would a fight with a lover suffice? It would have to, unless I could think of some other logical reason.

When the bus reached Las Delicias I was once again grateful to Doña Chuy. The town had a population of about twenty thousand people and ranches scattered around it. There would have been no opportunity to shop for clothes here. I was grateful for the designer jeans, sweaters and skirts Doña Chuy had purchased for me.

The clothes turned me into a modern day Mexican girl, albeit with white skin. This area was famous for its cheeses, and the influx of Mormons who had brought about that fame. The Mormons were of Nordic heritage so it wasn't unusual to see light-skinned Mexicans with blue eyes in this locale.

We found a Casa de Huespedes on the plaza, really primitive, but all right for the short time we planned to be there. Doña Chuy went out to buy herself a bus ticket and to arrange a cab to pick me up after dark.

The ranch was a good forty-five minute drive and I knew if I arrived at night, even if no family members were there, I wouldn't be turned away—Mexican hospitality. Doña Chuy's ticket was for the first bus out the following day. Her reasoning was that I would be able to get back to her at Las Delicias in case something should go wrong at the ranch.

The day passed quickly and we gave each other a tearful embrace and promised to keep in touch with each other. I pressed five hundred dollars in her hand. She, like El Pequeño, didn't want to accept it. I insisted. It was such a small amount for all of the trouble she had gone to for me. I laughingly told her to buy some pigs with it, and she could make me *carnitas* next time I came. This way we eased ourselves into the parting and I was in the taxi going to Villa Ahumada.

The driver was familiar with the rancho. He told me he had relatives that lived and worked at the hacienda. I answered his questions as briefly as possible, but in a way that led him to continue to talk. In this way, I hoped to find out what was going on there and who may or may not be there.

Chihuahua is large and there are many mountains, the most famous being the Sierra Madre as mentioned before. I remembered the time I was there with Dolores, seeing Tarahumara Indians running in their native dress. She had explained to me that they were known for their ability to run for miles without food. She had pointed out a little bag they carried on their belts. She said it contained *pinole*, a mixture of blue corn, pine nuts and brown sugar, ground together and put in these bags to be used as an energy source when they were running.

I remembered also another time we were slumming in Juárez during Easter vacation and had stopped to eat in a restaurant on the way back to the ranch. These Tarahumara Indians came up to the window of the restaurant staring in. They looked like something from another century.

19

THE RANCH

The road to the ranch was long, bumpy and dusty. At last we arrived at the entrance to the hacienda. The driver honked and someone came running to open the gate for us, after recognizing the driver. They explained that Don Ramón was in residence but he wasn't expecting anyone.

Don Ramón was Dolores' father. I knew he would accept my being there for whatever reason. He was waiting on the patio with open arms to embrace me and tell me once again, "*Mi casa es su casa.*"

He paid off the driver and led me into the library where there was a crackling fire going. He had been working on the ranch books, they were scattered around his desk. He rang the bell and ordered brandies and *botanas* for us. He wanted us to have a chance to talk before dinner. When the brandies were served and we had toasted each other's good health, he put his drink down and looked askance at me.

I rather shamefacedly told him I had had a quarrel with my fiancée and left in a fit of rage. I didn't tell him where I had left from and he didn't ask. He told me again I was welcome to stay as long as I wanted. He said if I had second thoughts I could invite my fiancée to join me at the ranch. He would be welcome also. This was real nobility. I knew he would protect me with his life, if need be.

We had another brandy. I asked about Dolores. He told me she was living in Chihuahua. Her husband managed one of the many industries they owned. He wanted to send her a message as there was no phone at the hacienda.

I begged off and told him I needed a few days of rest, then I hoped she could come for a few days and we could visit. He called me *pobre niña* and told me again that I had his protection as long as it was needed.

Juana the maid came in to announce dinner. She gave a great shout of joy and surprise at finding me there. I was beginning to feel more secure as the moments passed.

Don Ramón was a master host. He kept me entertained all through dinner with tales of business exploits, incidents on the ranch, and his travels with Doña Carmen, who this very minute was on her way to Spain. She had left the ranch early that morning. He told me how sorry she would be to have missed seeing me.

After an excellent dinner of stuffed Cornish game hens, fresh asparagus, avocado and orange salad and crusty Mexican bread, we went back to the library for a cognac and a game of backgammon.

Several games and a couple more cognacs later, I was ready for bed. He had beaten me three games out of five. I begged off, saying I was tired and a little *borracha*. I did promise to beat him at backgammon the next day.

He rang for Juana to show me to my room. He bade me good night and told me to sleep late. He said we would see each other at *comida*, the big meal of the day, usually served between two and four in the afternoon.

Juana kept up the chatter as we walked to my room. I knew, since there was no phone at the ranch and the closest town was about twenty miles away, that I would need Juana to get a message out. It was good to see her again after so many years but I overdid it a little because of my need of her. We talked for a few minutes with her buzzing around making sure I would be comfortable then, saying good night, she left.

There is something to be said for luxury, and having lived a few days without it, I was ready to wallow in it and never be without it again. I took a long leisurely bath.

My thoughts always returning to Enrique when I was alone, I wondered where he was, and if he was also running. Andrew could have had him picked up.

At this point in my isolation there was no use to speculate. I fell asleep wishing his arms were around me. I awoke hours later to the sounds of the house people stirring around getting ready for their days work. It was time to work on getting a message to Andrew.

I did some fond remembering thinking about Andrew that morning. I was just out of the FBI Academy and I had come before Andrew highly recommended by my now deceased uncle who had been a senator. Andrew had assigned me to work with an older agent by the name of Frank.

We were investigating a drug-related credit card fraud. I had done a good job under adverse circumstances. Frank, my partner was something of a womanizer, and he thought he could put his claim on me right away. I tolerated his ribald jokes, double meanings and an occasional pat on the butt. One day he went too far and left me in a precarious situation that could have gotten me killed. He was trying to prove I needed him and he wouldn't be there unless I put out.

I got out of the situation on my own and promptly sched-
uled a meeting with Andrew and Frank. He was so sure that I
would eventually succumb to him, he showed up at the meeting
with a smirk to let me explain how "we" had gotten out of the
situation.

I discussed the circumstances and explained how I had
gotten out of it on my own. I then told Andrew, in front of
Frank, that Frank was a male chauvinist pig. I gave Andrew a
documentation of every incident that had passed between the
two of us.

Frank denied it all and left in a huff, with egg on his face.
I told Andrew it might cost me my job, but I would no longer
work with Frank. I was twenty-four years old at the time and
scared to death of Andrew, the boss. Andrew defended my position and promptly found me another partner, Andy.

Andy was younger than Frank and not prejudiced against
women in the DEA. Andrew had kept his eye on me since that
time and had become a very good friend. He graded me as an
excellent agent and respected me. I knew him well enough to
know that he was conducting a thorough search for me and
would not give up until I was found. After Costa Rica, I knew
there was more to his feelings than professional, but I didn't
know how I felt about it.

As I bathed, I was thinking how lucky I was to get this far
on my journey back to the United States. I was more than half
way back. As I dressed, Juana came into the room with a tray
containing a pot of coffee, orange juice, and a sweet roll.

From my days visiting the ranch I remembered that she took
Saturday afternoon and Sundays off. I could have her place a call
to my Aunt Betty and wish her a happy birthday. I smiled and
told her how sweet it was of her to wait on me.

Then I went on, "Isn't it your afternoon off tomorrow?"

She was pleased that I remembered and asked me if I would like her to stay.

"Of course not, Juana," I replied. "You work too hard as it is. There is something you can do for me though, if you will."

"*Sí, señorita*," she said, "I will do anything for you."

I asked her if I gave her some money if she could place a telephone call to my aunt in Georgetown to wish her a happy birthday for me.

"I've always called her or visited on her birthday and I don't want her to think I've forgotten. I'll give you the number and you just say that you are calling for me. Explain that I am visiting on a ranch in Mexico that has no phone. Tell her I send birthday wishes and a great big kiss by you," I finished.

Juana was pleased that I would ask her to do this very important task. Families are so important in Mexico and she admired my attention to my aunt.

The telephone call would be a signal to my aunt to get in touch with Andrew. She would know, since it was not her birthday, that I needed assistance. He would trace the call and know I was alive and healthy, but in need of rescue. Today was Friday. I shouldn't have too long to wait for a message of some kind. On other assignments, messages had come in every form and way imaginable. Even though this was a very isolated spot, I did not doubt Andrew would either come or get a message to me.

At *comida* that day Don Ramón was all enthusiastic because he had to fly to Chihuahua Monday on business. He was making big plans to bring Dolores back with him. He wanted me to go with him but I begged off. I told him I was fighting off a cold, and if Dolores was coming with the children, I had better stay put and rest.

It was his habit to take a nap after *comida* so I found myself alone in the library. The solitude was good. I was enjoying the ranch as always, the soft desert colors at sunset with the Sierra Madre Mountains in the distance.

The ranch sounds were becoming familiar once again. I felt like the ranch had opened up its arms and enfolded me, making me comfortable and I almost wished I never had to leave the safety net I'd found here.

After spending the afternoon thinking I had been right to trust Juana, that she was my best messenger, Don Ramón came back to the library to find me. I had opened one of the books as window dressing and I hoped I looked relaxed and peaceful. He asked me if I felt up to some backgammon after a light dinner. I assured him I did.

The meal was refreshing as usual. There were just the two of us. He was anxious to get the game going. He really was good and always looking for a challenge. Something I could never refuse was a challenge. I suppose my being an only child is what made me have the desire to test my mettle at every opportunity. There were no siblings to take me down a peg.

Don Ramón and I carried on a lively conversation as we played. He was in high spirits and teased me about the lover that I had run away from. He jokingly wanted to know what my lover had done that made me so angry. He commented that if he were my lover he would be angry with me. When I asked why, he said for dying that beautiful red hair. I told him it was only dye and would grow out in a few months, but let him think it was something my love had done to me.

I beat him several games and drank cognac with him. The evening passed pleasantly and I excused myself and went once more to my room.

Juana took off at noon the next day, with my instructions and money to pay for a telephone call to the United States.

Don Ramón mentioned I would have to be cook and house-keeper for the weekend unless I wanted to drive into Las Delicias to eat. I told him I was looking forward to cooking for him and Juana had left her niece to do the cleaning while she was away.

I had already looked in the *dispensa* to decide what meals I would serve. Breakfast would be simple for the weekend but I planned an elaborate *comida* for both Saturday and Sunday evening. I felt like I was earning my keep and enjoyed the op-portunity to do something for Don Ramón in exchange for his hospitality. Someday I would have to let him know how much he had done for me.

Saturday, I made a leg of lamb marinated in a paste of sherry and ground almonds, and cooked over the rotisserie. I also made a lemon meringue pie knowing his fondness for sweets. Sunday, I made a simple dish from France called coq au vin, and a chocolate mousse for dessert. He had an inimitable collection of wines that could have put any host to shame. It was almost like a miracle in this isolated spot.

We went horseback riding Sunday morning up into the mountains a little way. He wanted to show me the parameters of the ranch. It was enormous: his grandfather had been given the ranch, during the time of Pancho Villa, as payment for his valor on the battlefield in the Revolution.

There had been several legal battles since that time to keep the ranch. During the time of Lázaro Cárdenas, they did, in fact, lose part of it because some of the land had been leased to an American oil company. Don Ramón knew his Mexican his-tory and was very diverting. There were times I actually forgot why I was there.

The time passed quickly and Monday was there. Don Ramón flew off to Chihuahua to get his business done quickly and bring Dolores back. I was looking forward to her visit, but I was thinking about how quickly Andrew would receive my message and mobilize to get me out of Mexico. Juana had passed on my message.

Dolores and I had a great reunion. Don Ramón had not told her I was at the ranch. She was really surprised, me being the last person in the world she expected. He told her he was lost without her mother and begged her to come and stay a few days. She had a set of twin boys and an adorable little girl. Don Ramón doted on the boys. I had the feeling he had never said no to them.

We spent most of Monday night catching up on each other's lives. She met and married a *chilango*, as people from Mexico City are called by the people from other states in Mexico. She went on to tell me what a good father and husband he was and like a son to her father. She said she was sorry business had kept him in Chihuahua, but maybe he would come on Wednesday.

She kind of looked askance at me, as if to say "What are your plans? How long will you be staying?"

I knew I owed her an explanation as to why I was there, and of course how long I would be staying. The ranch wasn't just some place one would stop in passing through, and especially without a car. I supposed she and her father had discussed this. I told her something of Enrique and said I was on an assignment that had involved him and I had decided to run out on it the last minute.

Before she could ask, I told her I couldn't explain further except that I was waiting for a connection with my boss. I told her he would be in touch with me any day now.

The newspapers Don Ramón brought back were filled with stories of the big bust that occurred in the Caymans. I could only hope we were far enough away that she didn't make the connection. She assured me I was welcome and we went back to talking about mundane things. It was difficult because my mind kept going back to the terror I felt when I saw the helicopter with the presidential seal on top of a building, waiting for Enrique to board.

I realized then, in the game that was being played out, I was only a minor player. Although my information had brought it about, I was most definitely expendable.

20

THE SEARCH IS ON

I hadn't seen Matt, or whatever his name was, for a few days. The chance of my meeting him again was positively assured. My arrest had been pretty close in the Caymans. Natalie was the reason I hadn't been busted. Evidently their plan was to bring her out first. My politician friends had apparently escaped for the time being.

The feds needed a witness to put us all together. It would take an idiot not to know their witness was Natalie. All the clues were there from the beginning, but I had been in love like a school boy, blind to everything else.

My partners let me know the heat was mine. I had created the problem and they expected me to take care of it. If I couldn't get to Natalie first, I probably wouldn't live to face a trial.

An alternative plan was in my head. I had started dismantling my illegal operation. The task of destroying records and moving money had already been completed. I had several sets of paperwork for false identities; however, all of them had been used by me at one time or another, and were known to my business associates. I felt like I was stranded alone. Everything I did from now on must be to hide from everyone around me, people I was more accustomed to dealing with openly.

The day before, while I had been in Guadalajara, taking care of legitimate pharmaceutical business, I called Luis into my office and assigned him a job that would occupy him for a couple of hours.

After that I had my secretary place a telephone call to my doctor. I chatted with him for a while about getting together for a weekend soon on the Elena. When I hung up I told my secretary I had made myself a doctor's appointment and would be out of the office for an hour or so.

From the office I drove to a church, three miles away. The resident priest was my cousin, Saúl. I asked for an audience outside the confessional. After I made a good size donation and many promises to remain as legal as he was for the remainder of my life, he agreed to contact a mutual acquaintance for me and purchase passports, birth certificates and a marriage certificate for a man and his wife.

It was all arranged and I could pick them up at the church in two days. I would put the pictures on them myself. No one but Saúl would know the new names.

In the meantime I had to breathe some new life into the search. No trace had been found in any direction. We had searched buses, trains, boats and airports to no avail. I had men stationed at all border crossings.

I knew someone else had been searching for Natalie since she had disappeared and I suspected it was the DEA. Evidently they didn't have her or know where she was hiding. This little *señorita* was on her own.

She had eluded us all for days, but I knew time was getting short. Natalie would know I would be looking for her and the DEA would be in the game. What she possibly did not realize is how long the arms of the Mexican and United States politicians can stretch. Crooked politicians always have many friends because they can afford to pay very well for favors. They wanted her dead. There wasn't a witness protection program anywhere that would help her. We were talking about very powerful vicious men. I had been witness to this in my business associations with them. I was never afraid of them because we were on the same side. My position had drastically changed.

21
NEGOTIATIONS

I called and set up a meeting with Enrique. Probably the only reason he went along with meeting me was because I told him I knew where Natalie was hiding and I felt we needed to talk. Fear of being arrested didn't deter him, I'll give him that.

We agreed to meet at the La Destilería Restaurant in the bar at 9.00pm on the night I telephoned him. He asked me how he would know me.

I had introduced myself over the phone as Andrew Martin, from the United States Drug Enforcement Agency. Knowing he probably recognized my voice, I replied, "You'll know me."

Of course he did. He walked up and smiled down at me sitting in the agreed-upon back booth.

"How are you, Matt?" he said, as he took my outstretched hand. Sliding into the booth facing me, he asked, "Are you her boss?"

"More than that," I replied, "I am her boss and a very good friend."

"I wouldn't brag about being her boss." He was suddenly angry. "You have put her in a hell of a lot of danger, and not necessarily from me."

"I know that," I said. "That's why I wanted us to meet."

It was hard for me to tell Enrique Natalie had confessed to me she loved him and wasn't sure she would be able to turn him in. I knew by the look in his black eyes, it was the only good news he had had in days.

"Why are you telling me this?" he asked.

I watched him intently as I answered. "With love comes responsibility. I love her enough to come to you because she loves you. My gut feeling is that you are in love with her. One of us has to save her. What we need to decide is which one can do the best job of protecting her. You know the dangers as well as I do. Are you willing to put her first and cooperate with me to save her life?"

A long silence followed. I think I shocked him being so blunt. Maybe he was deciding if he could trust me. Finally he picked up his glass, took a long drink, and looked me straight in the eyes as he said a firm, "Yes." Then he continued, "I have made some plans toward getting her out if I could find her. We better compare notes. There are probably at least a dozen contracts out on her. It's not going to be easy; in fact you may have to be the one. I may not live that long."

We sat in the booth for three hours throwing ideas back and forth and then digging holes in them all. He confided in me that he had new identifications ready to go for a man and wife. Reaching into his pocket, he pulled out a sheet of paper and handed it to me.

"Don't look at it now," he said. "I have placed enough money, clean money, into accounts in Natalie's name to last her a lifetime, just in case something happens to me. That sheet has all the information she will need to use it."

My instinct had been correct. He really did care for her and was ready to do what he could to see her escape. One of my agents had reported the instructions given by Enrique to his men, "Don't kill her; bring her to me." This made me believe I could trust him. I was pretty desperate.

Although I now knew where she was and was working on a plan to bring her out of Mexico, what could I do that would guarantee her safety in the United States? Enrique's money would help because it meant that no government money would have to be requested, or accounted for.

I told Enrique it would be a good idea for him to hide out for a few days and to keep in touch with me. I was going back to Washington early the next morning. I gave him numbers where he could reach me at all times. He knew something big was coming down.

We both agreed that the right plan had not been devised as yet and that it would be necessary for us to meet again, and soon. I told him that after a day or two in the States I would have a clearer picture as to what I could do.

22
NOBILITY

The nobility of man under fire can never be predicted. I had to ask Enrique the hard question and I didn't know what he would reply. Maybe I didn't even have the right to ask but, where Natalie's safety was concerned, I'd bend almost any rule. The back booth at La Destilería Bar was our home away from home, so to speak. We had met there on three occasions; this would be our fourth meeting.

We always planned for me to arrive first. If the situation didn't look good I would leave and telephone him. So far we had been lucky. None of the DEA agents in Mexico had any idea where Enrique was staying. He had very effectively disappeared but, true to his word, he had kept in touch with me. I really didn't want to know where he could be located. If asked, I didn't need to lie.

I had started my second drink when he showed. At first I didn't recognize him. He was dressed in old jeans and a blue work shirt. His hair was long on his neck. He wore an old dirty gray hat that hid his eyes. On his feet were well worn Mexican sandals. The booth where I sat was dark, an outside door right behind it. He slid in opposite me and offered his hand.

"How goes it, *compadre*?" he asked.

I could see the strain of the past few days on his face. I remembered his eyes when I had told him that Natalie had confessed her love for him. We each started speaking at once, the name Natalie on our lips. We smiled at each other, and I felt that the bond of mutual trust was growing stronger. We had a common goal: to save Natalie at all costs, and to save ourselves if possible. His danger came from his associates, as did mine. The long arm of the law reaches everywhere. I knew I was safe as long as the powers-that-be thought I put the government first. I did, but with one exception: Natalie.

These meetings with Enrique had shown me a side of him that made me aware of how Natalie could love him. He was a nobleman with honor and pride in who he was and what he was about. I discerned that he liked the excitement and danger of drug dealing and of course the wealth.

He confided that he had wanted out for a long time but couldn't break loose because he knew too much. It was because of his honor and integrity that he had been allowed to advance so quickly inside the drug cartel. His education, social skills and private business were all bonuses. I told him his knowledge might save him. I took a long drink and we looked at each other in silence. He knew something was coming.

"Enrique," I finally said, "It's time to separate the men from the boys. Are you willing to replace Natalie as a government witness if I guarantee you I will get her resettled in safety? I have a plan I will explain to you."

He never hesitated a moment, "You know I will. Whatever it takes. Right now, I don't feel like you, me, or anyone can save her from the jackals out there who feel betrayed by me, because of her. In fact they believe I already have her, and are demanding that I turn her over to them or they will kill me."

I smiled and said, "Let me explain my plan."

After a flight of no sleep and floor walking, I had come up with what I though was a pretty good idea.

"What if Natalie should get killed?" I asked.

His eyes became cold and dangerous.

"No, no," I said. "I mean we make it look like she is killed in an accident. We could arrange a fatal accident almost anywhere in Mexico. It could be car or boat, preferably near a border making it look as if she were trying to get back to the United States. Better yet, I could arrange for her name to be added to a list of victims that have already been in an accident. This would be even more convincing. There are so many traffic fatalities in Mexico each day that this would probably be the easiest to arrange. She is safe where she is. We could pick her up once the "accident" comes down."

I told Enrique that if we used his money the government agencies would not be involved and it would be easier to keep the secret.

Enrique thought it was a sound idea and possibly the only one we could pull off. He asked me how much money it would take to accomplish it. I told him and he said he would have that much money on him the next time we met. He told me he didn't want to know her new location.

"What I don't know can't be forced out of me," he finished.

We agreed he would give me all the information we needed as soon as Natalie was safe. The subject came around as to how he would be handled as a witness.

I told him we would need to take his deposition as soon as possible. The Vice President had instructed me to arrange for the deposition. He said he would have an attorney he could trust from the Justice Department fly in to take the deposition.

After much discussion we decided on a schedule we would attempt to keep.

I asked him if he could stay hidden for another couple of days. He assured me he could. I promised him I would have Natalie dead in the newspapers and on a plane to a new identity by that time.

We agreed, when it was accomplished, I would take a suite at the El Tapatío Hotel and we would meet in the La Diligencia Bar there at three o'clock in the afternoon. We planned for it to be on the third day from the current date. Enrique had felt that it would be a quiet time at the hotel and hopefully safe.

From the bar we would go upstairs and take the deposition. When the deposition was finished we planned to drive him to Manzanillo where a boat would be waiting to receive him. The destination of the boat we left indefinite for the time being. My thought, and I shared it with him, was to have the boat take him to an aircraft carrier and we would leave him aboard until he was needed. I knew the Vice President could arrange it through the Secretary of Defense.

Fate made it a little easier that afternoon, there was a car-bus wreck outside of Orizaba, a little mountain town not far from Puebla. Natalie's name appeared as one of the victims. The newspaper article read that an American tourist had been killed along with two children and a male adult. It was arranged on a local level and to let the news out would have gotten the officials in a lot of trouble. It cost me big time but was worth every penny.

23

RESCUE

I soon realized the airport was not the place for me to start the journey to rescue Natalie. I remembered a minor drug-dealing informer that lived close to the airport. I put two DEA agents into a taxi as a decoy, sending them to the airport. By the time they sat there for three hours and then returned to Tom's house, I could be far away.

I asked Poncho, the informer, to meet me at the Novales Hotel prepared for a trip. He knew this favor would be returned ten-fold, and was eager to oblige. I had him drive me to Monterey. This would help obliterate my trail if I was being followed.

Poncho left me at the airport thinking I was flying to the States. I took a taxi from there and had it take me all the way to Torreón, pretending I had an urgent appointment there. Upon arriving in Torreón I got yet another taxi to Las Delicias.

From there I hired a car to take me to the ranch. The dusty, bumpy roads seemed to go on forever.

Our meeting was emotional but reserved. We couldn't ask each other too many questions until we were alone. Don Ramón soon saw that we needed time alone. After offering me a drink, he excused himself.

We went into the library. Natalie was nervous with a thousand questions in her eyes. I played the boss once again although it was breaking my heart to see her in this state. She had been through an ordeal, no doubt about that, and I would be asking her to go through yet another trauma. I was stern. I asked that she allow me to do the talking and told her our plan. I told her that I had been with Enrique.

"Between the two of us we have a developed a plan to save your life. I trust Enrique. He has put his life on the line for you and wants you to accept what he is doing."

When I told her about him already having false identifications and a marriage license ready before I began my talks with him, she smiled.

We spoke of our various meetings, mine and Enrique's. I let her know that he was in danger from his own people because he would betray them and put his trust in her.

I explained that, in spite of the danger, he had arranged for large sums of clean money to be placed in the name we had selected for her, enough to last her a lifetime if anything happened to him. I let her know that very powerful people were looking for her on both sides of the border. Then I broke the news that for all intents and purposes she had been killed in a bus wreck outside of Orizaba.

I brought out a new passport I had had made for her in the name of Nicole Favier, a French passport. I said she would be going to France to live for a long while. Then I told her I had been in touch with her Aunt Betty and she had arranged for her to stay with a friend of hers in Chamonix.

Our next plan was to get her out of here, in case there was anyone still looking for her in Mexico. I thought it was time to involve Don Ramón in our plans, and she agreed. She went to look for him and I breathed a sigh of relief that she had accepted it so readily.

When she and Don Ramón came back I busied myself mixing us a drink, to give me time to approach him. He waited patiently knowing this wasn't some minor situation we were involved in. Natalie started by telling him she hadn't been completely honest. I interrupted by taking out my badge and explaining the predicament we were in.

He didn't hesitate a minute to offer his assistance. He told Natalie once again how much she meant to him and Dolores, and that he would do anything possible to help us. I didn't feel it pertinent to tell him about the forged passport, but asked him if he could fly Natalie to Belize, so she could get a flight to Europe. I asked that it be as soon as possible. He said he could have his plane ready and in the air within the hour.

I hated to leave her so soon because I felt she needed reassurance but I also needed to keep my appointment with Enrique. I had a big score to settle in Washington and must get the ball rolling. I asked Don Ramón for time alone with Natalie while the plane was being readied. I told him I needed to give her further instructions and it was agreed that they would take off at 6.00pm. I would head back to Guadalajara.

It was hard for Natalie to comprehend all that I was saying. She had been through so much. At last I wrote it all down, thinking it would be better to see it in writing. There was no doubt that the amount Enrique had left her was impressive. She wouldn't have to start her new life by pinching pennies, a long way from it, but she would have to live modestly and discreetly to avoid unwanted attention. My goodbye to her was tender and I promised as soon as things settled down I would come to her and tell her all that happened.

We were both a little teary as she climbed aboard the plane. I grasped Don Ramón's hand and told him I trusted him with the most important person in the world to me. He just nodded his head, he understood. When I could no longer see the plane, I walked back to the garage and into the waiting car that Don Ramón had provided for me to start my journey to the airport.

24

NICOLE FAVIER

Don Ramón was the same caring companion I had spent the last week with, except for the fact that there seemed to be an awareness about him. Maybe I just hadn't noticed it before. My mind was a myriad of thoughts, flashing in and out, trying to concentrate on what lay ahead for me. I felt I could face most anything because Enrique still loved me and had tried so hard to see that I was safe.

Chamonix was a ski resort and not too far from the French Riviera. I knew I would be safe there.

Tante Isabelle would be happy to see me. I hadn't seen her since the summer I was thirteen when I went there with Aunt Betty.

Andrew and I had agreed that, after a month or so there, I should fly to the clinic in Berne, Switzerland, for minor surgery, definitely a nose job and maybe a different cast for the eyes. Oh, the days of miracle surgery, but these little differences could save my life.

From the moment I had gotten on the plane I was Nicole Favier. There was a sadness in me for that persona, Natalie. I almost cried at the thought of what my parents and Aunt Betty would be going through.

Andrew had told me Aunt Betty would go to my parents and tell them that, if they wanted me to live, they must pretend that I had died, and then convince people of that fact with grieving, a memorial service, and the whole thing.

When we reached the airport in Belize, Don Ramón and I had a poignant parting. We promised each other to one day have a horseback ride again on the ranch and a good game of backgammon. He told me I had been his fiercest opponent. I thanked him again and told him I would be forever in his debt.

He said, with tears in his eyes, "You are my American daughter."

As I landed in Paris I was thinking of Mirelle, *Tante* Isabelle's niece. How proud the aunts had been when we had met that summer of thirteen and had become instant friends. Our summer had been spent trying on each other's clothes and talking about boys, the difference between French and American men, as if we knew.

I only had the few clothes that Doña Chuy had bought for me in Torreón. I decided if I stayed low key it would be safe for me to shop for a few essentials. I also needed to make arrangements for the money investments Enrique had given me. The major portion of it I would leave in Switzerland but I needed some for living expenses in France. I needed a strong box for most of the jewels, and a checking account for the hundred thousand dollars Andrew had given me. For now the decisions would be mine. I knew it would be a few weeks or months before I saw Andrew again and possibly years before I saw Enrique or my parents.

After a couple of days of shopping I was ready for Chamonix. Paris didn't seem the same alone and there was no one I could call on. Andrew had advised me to take a train out of

Paris, which I did. As he directed I bought a ticket to a small village several miles from Chamonix and then took a taxi back to Chamonix. I had the taxi driver leave me at the train station and took a bus across town and then another taxi to *Tante* Isabelle's home.

She welcomed me with a strong hug and kiss on each cheek. She had aged, but somehow the French women seem to keep that "chic" look right into old age. The chateau was beautiful, large and comfortable with a magnificent view of the mountains. She, like Aunt Betty, had her old retainers and a pert little maid from the village. My room was luxuriously furnished in French country style, with a fire burning brightly to make it look welcoming. I knew this was only temporary lodging, but it felt like a haven and I once again felt safe.

25

ASSASSINATION

I had been able to move around fairly well because I had been invisible during the actual busts. Today I had taken the precaution of having back up. Two armed men were in the hotel suite with the attorney. I had my two best men watching my back as I walked into the bar. Two other men were stationed in the lobby to pick up on anyone following Enrique.

We met in the bar as planned. We ordered drinks to avoid suspicion. Enrique looked harassed. He was back in his own clothes. I was sure pride kept him from showing up for his deposition in dirty Levi's.

We didn't talk until the drinks were delivered.

"Is she safe?" he asked.

"Yes," I replied. She's out of Mexico and not in the United States. No one knows where she is, except me."

"Gracias," he said softly. "Now maybe I can sleep. None of the rest of it is important."

We quickly finished our drinks, saying very little.

Taking the elevator up to the fifth floor we talked about the mechanics of the deposition. I left two men downstairs in the lobby. The two following me would be in the hotel room inside a closet.

Once inside the suite it all came together. He had brought an attaché case filled with paperwork which detailed records of times, places and people. The attorney took possession of the case. He told Enrique that if he was ready they should start the deposition. Enrique smiled and said, "Let the games begin."

Enrique and I were both nervous. It couldn't have been easy for him to turn against everyone he had known in his dark business, because they were also social friends. He knew he was saving himself from dying, but that he would lose a lot of his wealth and probably do some prison time. I had assured him I would do everything in my power to get him the best deal possible, but I couldn't promise no prison time. He understood. It was saving Natalie that had made him decide to do this.

When we were forty-five minutes into the deposition, and all feeling pretty good about the powerful evidence Enrique was giving us, the hotel room door broke open with the staccato sounds of machine gunfire. Enrique fell to the floor. I knew he was hit. The rest of us also hit the floor. Thank God I had brought back-up. They burst from the closet and killed the gunmen.

I ran to Enrique, who lay on his side, and turned him over. The entire front of his body was riddled with bullet holes. A deep sadness hit me as I closed his eyes. Knowing there was nothing more I could do for him, I grabbed the tape recorder and the attaché case and went into the connecting suite of rooms. The others followed. Once the door was closed, I surveyed the other three men. Jim, the attorney had been hit in the shoulder. No one else had been hit. It was very evident who they meant to kill.

We couldn't afford to be picked up anywhere near this scene or the attaché case would be confiscated and we would be jailed. Tony, one of the agents, checked outside the window and all was quiet so far. The other agent, Bob, walked down the corridor to the service elevator, propped it open, and came back for us. We had put a towel to Jim's shoulder and I gave him my jacket. His bloody one we took along with us, doubled up inside the attaché case.

Once down the stairs and outside we walked down the street a little way and caught a passing cab. As we drove away, police cars were screaming to a stop in front of the hotel. I had the cab driver take us to a doctor across the city. Jim was patched up and I left him in the care of the well paid doctor, with Bob as guard. I figured the cash would keep the doctor quiet long enough for Jim and Bob to get out of the country. Tony and I headed for the airport for a plane going anywhere in the United States. Enrique had given his life to give us this evidence. I would guard it with mine.

26

LUIS FONSECA

No one in the organization seemed to know where to find Enrique. I was afraid to ask too many questions. Enrique had gotten all of us in a real mess. I knew Enrique had girl friends in the past and no way would I inform my sister that Enrique was the money man and I was on his team. From the time Natalie had come on the scene he had been like a different person. He wouldn't listen to anyone who attempted to tell him to be cautious of her.

I was really worried now that she was missing. She was probably going to give all of us up and that meant a long prison term for me. I was in the lake house in Ajijic trying to hold the fort together. Everyone wanted to talk to Enrique and I was sure they didn't believe the lame excuses I gave for his absence.

This had been going on for three days. It was late in the afternoon of the third day and I had almost decided I should talk to my sister, Elena, and tell her at least that there might be a problem. She didn't know anything about Enrique's business and could not have cared less. As long as the money was there to spend when she wanted it, it made no difference to her where it came from. I knew Elena was back in Mexico City. Our parents also lived there. I wanted to have the helicopter pilot fly me up there but I was afraid Enrique might get back and want to use it.

The cook had served me a light meal and I had had as many drinks as I felt I could handle. Enrique never over indulged and he didn't like it in his people when they were on duty.

I had walked outside and was talking to the helicopter pilot when one of the gardeners ran up to us and said, "Policía! Policía!"

Fear gripped me but I knew I had to cover for Enrique. I walked back into the house and waited for them to be brought before me. They were not local police but came from Guadalajara, eight officers in all. The one who had designated himself spokesman asked me who I was.

"Luís Fonseca, the brother-in-law of Enrique Vázquez," I answered. He asked me a few questions about who lived in the house with Enrique. I told him it was one of several homes belonging to Enrique and that, at the present time, the only family staying here was Enrique and myself.

"Where is Mr. Vázquez's wife?" was his next question.

I answered, "She is visiting our parents in Mexico City."

There was no attempt made to soften the news. "Mr. Vázquez has been murdered this afternoon in Guadalajara," he said.

I was so jolted I tried to stand and couldn't make it. My voice didn't work. After several attempts to talk failed, he began to give me the details as he knew them. He asked me to notify Enrique's wife. He then directed me to call the morgue and give them instructions as to what the family wanted done with the body.

They excused themselves and I sat lower and lower in the chair until my head was on the desk. I cried like a baby.

Three hours later I arrived at the home of my parents, by helicopter. Elena was not at home. She had gone to a cocktail party at a local club and was not expected home until late. My parents received the news. Not wanting them to know the nature of the business Enrique and I had been involved in, I said in answer to their questions I had no idea who had killed him or why.

My father, ever protecting of his little girl, did not want Elena to hear the news around a crowd of people, so he said we would wait. I fixed us the drink we all needed and we sat down to await her return. I found it ironic that her social life had so affected her marriage to Enrique and now news of his death had to wait for her social activity to end. No wonder Natalie was so important to him, I thought to myself.

27

MIGUEL

Sometimes the dream is better than the reality, Miguel was thinking, as he was finishing another back-breaking morning on the tractor. He had gone home to Monterrey as requested by Enrique. He was aware that Enrique would not soon forget the news he had given him regarding Natalie.

However, he still felt he had not been right to let her go. His deciding factor in letting her go had been the fact that she was just doing her job. Maybe this one time her heart had gotten in the way. He would always believe she loved Enrique. Maybe he was just a romantic.

He missed the soft life he had had while working with Enrique. He couldn't forget the generosity which had allowed him to buy the cattle ranch. Indeed he felt lucky to have found one so quickly.

More and more ranchers seemed to be giving up and moving into the cities in search of work. Lack of capital to see them through the bad years was a major factor.

His dream of owning a ranch was realized because of one such rancher. The reality of never ending work and the breeding of stock was sometimes more than he bargained for. He found himself wishing things could be as they were.

You cannot go backwards. Selina and the boys loved the ranch. Their support was heartwarming. Miguel knew he had the best of the two worlds. The drug business was not something he wanted his sons involved in. Selina was proud of their big rambling house. For the first time she had two servants to help her in the house.

His thoughts of Enrique and Natalie were ever in the back of his mind. He wanted them to be well and together, but didn't see this as a possibility. He and Enrique had both been fooled by Natalie. She was very good at her job. He couldn't fault her for that. Not knowing how much she had found out, maybe he should be worried but he knew she would never betray him. He had given her the opportunity to escape and she would do the same for him.

One more round on the tractor and he would go in for *comida*. He would listen to the news and might be able to pick up on what was happening. Enrique had made it clear he wanted no further contact with him so no news filtered down from that source. No news was good news but every day he expected it to break.

Miguel was hungry and the smell of fresh baked bread hung in the air as he outside the kitchen door in a pan kept there for that purpose. Giving Selina a hug and a kiss, he went to turn on the radio, kept on a shelf above the table. This was routine. Five minutes later, as Selina served him a big plate of food, came the news he had been dreading.

There had been a big drug bust. One of the drug kingpins had been murdered by his own associates. People were shocked to learn the drug king pin was Enrique Vázquez. Miguel hung his head; tears wet his cheeks and dropped into his food. Where was Natalie when she heard the sad news, he wondered? He remembered the times they had run the beaches and how she had laughed with him.

Enrique had been his friend since childhood. Maybe if he had believed Hoffman, Enrique would be alive today. He had been so sure Hoffman was suffering from acute paranoia.

The voice of the newsman caught Miguel's attention again. Evidently the death of a young American woman killed in a car accident a few days ago could be somehow related to the drug bust. It had become known, since her death, she was a DEA agent. Her name was Natalie.

Miguel's eyes teared again as he turned off the radio. They are together, he stated to himself. He would remember them that way and he would close the chapter on his other life. Thanks to Enrique, he was a rancher.

28

LE BIJOU

It seemed but a dream, the short time I had spent with Enrique. I was proud of him for giving testimony to spare me the ordeal and perhaps even my life. It would be a long time before I saw him again and maybe never. I had been responsible for bringing his empire down and changing his life.

After years in prison he might not want to see me again. His children would suffer the most. If I could think of a way to be supportive of them, while he was away, I would do so. They had their mother and Enrique's mother. Right at that moment I had a strong feeling that they would never even meet me or know how much I loved their father.

As I sat in the chateau watching the dying embers in the fireplace, I knew I had to come to terms with myself. As Andrew had said, start a new life. Although *Tante* Isabelle was a wonderful and gracious hostess, I needed a home of my own and soon. As we sat down to dinner that evening, I questioned her about the housing situation in the area. She told me again I was welcome to stay as long as I wished.

She said she was a lonely old woman and enjoyed my sharing her home. I detected sincerity and real affection in her voice, as well as truth.

She was lonely. It wouldn't be fair for me to stay long enough for her to accept my being there as part of her routine. I would visit often but I wanted to have my own privacy and a life in my own home.

The very next morning I telephoned an agent, recommended by *Tante* Isabelle, and set out to find myself a house. I still had Switzerland and surgery hanging over my head but I felt getting settled and being on my own came first.

Chamonix is a beautiful town and is quiet most of the year. The exception is the ski season. The economy in France was stable but the Second World War had taken its toll on the very rich. Lifestyles had changed for them as well as in other European countries. The upkeep on a house in a resort area, just to come and stay a few months a year, was no longer practical for the frugal Frenchman.

The agency showed me several chateaus but most of them were way too large. The money Enrique had put at my disposal could easily have taken care of such a lavish home but I had no intention of spending more than needed.

I kept thinking of the little *casita* that I had left behind in Ajijic. The memories of that little house, filled with flowers Enrique had sent me, and the sound of the waves on the shore of the lake, were tender and important to me. I could still see the women gathered with their Saturday wash standing on the edge of the shore. I couldn't let it go.

I finally got through to the agent that I wanted something smaller and not so baroque. In the late afternoon we stopped at the bottom of a lane that led up the mountain side. He explained that walking up the lane we would find a cottage that had long been in disuse. Almost the entire family that had owned the cottage had been put into concentration camps and eventually killed by the Nazis. The present owner lived in Paris. His intention was to sell the cottage. I had found my home.

It was a small chateau with only two bedrooms, a den, living room, only seven rooms in all. It had a coach house at the entrance nestled in thick pine trees. Even though it had been in disuse for many years, I immediately saw the possibilities. The coach house would be a perfect little place for a couple who could "do" for me. It would require some major cleaning but seemed to be strongly built.

The chateau walls were of aged brick with ivy climbing thereon. It was French country style, elongated beveled windows, fireplaces in each room and a magnificent view. I stood at one of the windows admiring the view and thought of the French custom of naming their homes. I would call mine, Le Bijou, which means the jewel in French. I could feel my enthusiasm for life returning. I had something to look forward to each day. I would repair and rebuild this chateau and make myself a home.

We made an agreement for an appointment the next day to close the deal. I felt like running back to *Tante* Isabelle to tell her what I had done. She could see the glow of my happiness the moment I walked in the front door. It was sad for her but she squared her shoulders and shared in my joy. I assured her I would be a frequent visitor at her home and that I would entertain her often in mine. She bustled around to serve us some tea and called François, her maid, in to give us some suggestions as to whom I could hire to take care of me.

I spent the next few days getting a contractor and shopping the stores for my new home. There were several antique stores in town and I invaded each one of them. The contractor *Tante* Isabelle had suggested was excellent. He had a flair for restoring, and I could soon see that he would turn my house into a showplace and deserving of the name Le Bijou.

We made plans to repair, paper, polish and upholster until it looked new, but old. There were quite a few good pieces of furniture, certainly well worth repairing. Although I only brought jewels and a few clothes with me, between the antique stores and the one local department store I could buy everything I needed for the time being.

I worked alongside the contractor and the cleaning people I had hired. It felt good to be busy but I seemed to lack physical strength. I tired easily. I thought I might have picked up a bug in Mexico. After a couple of weeks, I decided that, since the contractor had several more weeks of work, it might be a good time for me to go to Switzerland. It had been almost two months since I came to France.

Andrew would be expecting me to arrive at the clinic any day. I had not spoken to Andrew but we had agreed in Mexico, as I prepared to leave, that the clinic would be the best place for Andrew to contact me, since I was not sure of where I would be otherwise. It made sense to me to let the doctor at the clinic tell me if I had picked up a bug. They would have to give me a physical before performing surgery.

Tante Isabelle was eager and willing to keep an eye on my crew. Her enthusiasm had grown until it almost matched mine. I also made a plan to stop in Paris on my way and shop for linens, dishes, pots and pans and other things I would need for Le Bijou. I also wanted to get a small car that I could drive myself. I had always been self-sufficient and hated the idea of having to depend on someone when I wanted to go somewhere.

The clinic was, as I had anticipated, a large white sterile building surrounded by little cottages and a central dining room and living room. These areas were used for the patients and their guests to meet for pre-dinner drinks to entertain or to be entertained. There was a message waiting in my room that Andrew had called several days before and would be calling back on a daily basis until I entered the clinic.

As I was dressing for my doctor's appointment, he telephoned again. It was a brief call. He stated that he was in Milan, Italy, and would be flying in in two days' time. Our conversation was stilted, like people get when they haven't seen each other for a while, as if there may have been a change, the intimacy gone.

To my surprise, the doctor was a Russian. His accent was charming. His appearance was striking, a very large man with the clearest blue eyes I had ever seen. I felt immediate rapport with him. We exchanged small talk about my trip, the weather, etc., and then he rang for the nurse and asked her to get me undressed.

He gave me a routine examination and ordered several tests. I had told him about general lassitude, depression and weight loss. He thought a good endocrinology work-up should be the first priority. He told me that if I had a problem, it would be treated first by another doctor. His patients needed to be well and rested before he started any procedure. He advised me that test results were quickly received at the clinic.

He smiled as he said, "Money talks."

After a siesta in the afternoon, I was ready for company. I spent a good deal of time trying to decide what to wear. I sensed that it would be formal. The Europeans take eating seriously. They like to indulge all of the senses at one time. I wasn't wrong. The men had on dinner jackets. The women, who far outnumbered the men, were also dressed formally. I was glad that I had worn the emerald ring Enrique had given me.

It was nice to find some of the medical staff interspersed with the patients, among them my handsome doctor. I found myself comparing this small dinner to the party at Liz Byrnes' home in Ajijic and its group of bored women looking to temporarily latch on to someone for company. Circumstances had turned me into one such person. I could feel myself gravitating toward my doctor, Dr. Simikov. My ego let myself think he might be doing the same.

29

ANDREW

Two months had passed since I had seen Natalie aboard the plane for Belize. The five politicians, suspects in the drug operation, had all resigned, including the president. Very little of the drug money had been recovered. I doubted if it ever would be. The whole affair was too top secret to allow us to make the right inquiries.

Eight days after the president had resigned he died, presumably of a heart attack. Only the CIA Director and the now president knew all the facts.

I had been dreading the trip to Switzerland, at the same time wanting it, like breathing. Natalie had to be told of Enrique's death. There would be a period of mourning. At times the depression I felt over his death was still with me. He was a courageous man. Her grief would be private; she was that kind of woman. At times I was impatient for her to know so that the healing could begin. I just didn't like being the messenger. Hopefully her life in France would help because it was new and they had not spent time together there. She wouldn't be confronted with memories everywhere she went.

My plane reservations were a week away. I planned to be with her for two weeks. If it was necessary for me to stay longer, I would. She needed my compassion and my love as a friend. Hopefully at some time in the future she would need me as the number one person in her life.

After getting to know Enrique, I came to appreciate the man, and how she could have fallen in love with him. It didn't make it any easier for me. I had no intention of letting her retreat forever into a private place where love was not allowed to come again. Our relationship had a solid foundation. We had begun to build on friendship when Enrique came along. After a time, I felt we would be able to start the building process again.

My vacation would begin as soon as I took care of a matter in Milan, Italy. The United States Government had a good crew of DEA men and women in the office in Milan. One of them wanted to talk to me about transferring into the San Francisco office when his tour of duty was up in Milan. I had agreed to see him in the office in Milan since I was headed for Europe on my vacation.

It took the first week to clean up my desk. Feelings were beginning to come my way that my time in San Francisco might be coming to an end. Every few days I received a call from either the Director of the Justice Department or the Director of the CIA. They always requested meetings in isolated spots; there were always questions about the ordeal we had been through.

They appeared to me to be scared to death of a leak. It was as if they thought I needed to be reminded of the cost to the credibility of our country if anything leaked out. Recently, they had both been wanting to know if I would feel more comfortable in another job, maybe even a foreign assignment.

At first I was annoyed that my professionalism might be in question. Lately, I began looking forward to a change if it was coming. I was a worry to them. I had realized that being the only member of that ten-person team who wasn't elected to the position or politically appointed would be a detriment to me.

30

NATALIE

Andrew would be arriving the next day. I felt almost desperate to know what was going on. We had decided in our brief conversation that he would stay with me in my suite at the clinic. The suites had two bedrooms in case a patient wanted company. You have to remember that this was a clinic for the very rich. Every convenience had been considered. We had also decided I would not meet Andrew at the airport. I didn't know when my test results would be back and Dr. Simikov would want to talk with me about them.

After an evening of pleasantries and superficial conversation, I was ready for bed. There was something going on in my body that was making me ill. I attributed my illness to my concern for Enrique. Hopefully whatever bug I had picked up wouldn't delay the surgery. Maybe Andrew could set my mind at rest when he came.

I awoke the next day with a sense of expectation. It would be so good to see someone from home, especially Andrew. I had just finished dressing when my phone rang. He had arrived and they were bringing him to my suite. I had dressed very carefully and used more make up than I ordinarily did, in an attempt to hide my anxiety. It had taken its toll on my face and I had dark circles under my eyes and had lost about ten pounds of weight.

A light knock on the door and I swung it open and practically knocked him over with my arms encircling his waist. He hugged me back and we held each other without talking until we could bear to let go. Our rapport was such that once we began to talk it was as if we had seen each other only yesterday. However, a lot of water had gone under the bridge. I pulled him into the room and led him to a sofa where we both sat down.

He told me I needed to be patient and let him go through what had happened in the order that it had occurred. He began his story by telling me about going back to Guadalajara once again to see Enrique and tell him I was safely on my way to an undisclosed destination.

Enrique had agreed to a plea bargain, and to give testimony as a federal witness. They began by setting up a deposition. He said it was set up in the El Tapatío Hotel. They videotaped the deposition. Enrique had given them forty-five minutes of dates, names and places.

At this point in Andrew's narration, he put his arm around my shoulders and looked at me with the saddest, most serious look I had ever seen in his eyes. I knew what was coming. Then he proceeded to tell me the details of Enrique's death. I think I had always known this was the way our relationship would end, but I had thought I would be the one to die.

"Which side killed him?" I wanted to know.

"The drug czars," he replied.

Andrew believed that after they read of my death they must have decided they would get rid of Enrique in case he was planning to testify.

Andrew was such a comfort. He was tender and sensible at the same time. He held me in his arms and let me cry. His comforting words made sense to me even in my grief. After giving me a few minutes to pull myself together, he began his narration again, knowing I would want to hear it all.

He told me how the group had decided to quietly assassinate the president shortly after his resignation. I was really shocked. Andrew said that even he believed that the president couldn't be allowed to live, with him knowing all of the country's secrets, and him having a criminal mind. At any time he could have sold us out to a foreign country, probably to the highest bidder. It would leave our country too vulnerable.

Andrew told me that Enrique had not died in vain. He had been minutes away from the end of the deposition and his testimony had been clear and precise. The video of the deposition had convinced all five suspects in the government to resign and sign documents declaring their guilt. These documents would be used against them if they ever tried to run for public office again.

Then he told me it was time for him to confess a real trauma, one that had left him weak and unstable. This was the experience of helping my Aunt to make the arrangements for my funeral and a memorial. My death had been made much of in Washington and carrying out the natural sequence of my "death" helped to reinforce it in people's minds.

He said it had become so real to him at one point that he had to fight himself to stay off a plane headed for France to see for himself I was really alive. I could see love in Andrew's eyes as he spoke, but he only comforted me and spoke not a word of his own feelings beyond what he had said.

It was late afternoon before we were talked out. We had missed lunch but I felt like I would never be hungry again. I urged Andrew to go to the dining room and eat but he said he would call for a pot of coffee instead. Someone intervened in the kitchen and the tray arrived with not only coffee but sandwiches and cookies.

When I told Andrew I was expecting the doctor to call me in, he said the doctor knew I had had bad news. He assured me there would be no doctor's appointment that day unless I felt the need for a sleeping pill or a sedative. I said I didn't want anything. Andrew insisted that I lie down and try to sleep, if not, at least to rest. He tucked me in and let me know he would be in the next room if I wanted him.

My tears began again as the door closed. In my heart I felt I had known he was not alive. I had not felt him since I left Mexico. All the time I was running it was as if he would appear at any moment. In France he had never been with me.

We had dinner in the suite and talked again. Andrew mixed me a drink and afterwards I went to bed. Andrew was up during the night checking on me. At one point he held me after a very real nightmare had left me shaken and in tears. When morning came, after the long, long night, he insisted I go with him into the dining room for breakfast. When I sat down a nurse appeared and said the doctor would see me at eleven o'clock that morning.

This time I did the insisting. I wanted Andrew to rest. He looked so tired and I knew he had not slept. I told him to go to bed and I would come back as soon as I finished with the doctor. He thought it would be a good idea to leave the clinic in the afternoon and have a late lunch somewhere then go for a long walk. I'm sure he wanted me to get tired enough to sleep.

The doctor talked to me for a while giving me his condolences on the death of my fiancée. He answered some of my questions concerning the ordinary length of time for a cosmetic surgery. I had decided before I left Chamonix that I didn't want to be away longer than a month if possible.

The doctor finally got around to the results of my medical tests. I was stunned at their findings. I could hardly think what to tell Andrew. The doctor and I both agreed it was not the time for cosmetic surgery.

Andrew had slept soundly but awakened at the sound of me returning. When he inquired about the doctor visit I informed him I had a minor medical problem that would have to be treated before a surgery could be performed. Taking this into consideration, I told him, I had decided not to bother with the surgery at all. I would just take my chances with the face I had.

I'm sure he thought Enrique's death was the reason for my decision. He didn't argue the point. He softly told me that he had two weeks of vacation coming and he was inviting himself to go home with me.

Those next two weeks were the strangest I had ever lived through: most of the time it seemed like we were a much-married couple. I cooked for him when Adele, my servant, would allow me in the kitchen.

He worked alongside the carpenters and picked me wild flowers. He held me when I cried. We listened to music until we were exhausted. We slept in separate beds but most nights he lay beside me until I was asleep.

Andrew let me know that he wasn't feeling comfortable in the San Francisco office. He said the last assignment had left a bitter feeling in him. He wanted to prepare me in case he decided to get out. No decisions had been made, and probably wouldn't be for a while, as he had many loose ends.

I spoke to him of my parents. He said they had insisted on a memorial service in Iowa as well as in Washington. My mom had told Andrew it would help the stunned friends with whom I had partied such a short time before. At that moment, I mourned my own death. I had come to terms with being Nicole the French girl, but I missed my other life. I was also sad that my short career was over. Love for my country made me want that life of aiding in the denouncement of drugs.

Sometimes we joked with each other. I reminded him of the famous movie star he had met in the dining room at the clinic. He, like everyone else, focused much attention on her. She was not only famous but extremely beautiful. Andrew could hardly believe she felt it necessary to have cosmetic surgery. I told him if she crooked her little finger, I'd lose my companion fast.

The two weeks passed all too quickly and the last evening was upon us. Andrew was so serious I knew he hated leaving me alone. He suggested I write a note to my Aunt Betty inviting her to come for a visit. He would personally deliver it.

Just before bedtime, Andrew told me that he was going to stay away from me for one year. He marked on my calendar the day he would return. He said he loved me with all his heart. He told me he had loved me for a long time but he realized I needed time to grieve for Enrique.

"I understand why you loved him. I did everything in my power to keep him safe. He was my friend," he said softly.

We didn't speak of Enrique again. I wrote the letter for Aunt Betty as Andrew suggested. She had never had children and over the years I had become the closest thing she had to a daughter. I knew she would start planning a trip the minute she received the letter. I told her about falling in love with Chamonix and what a charming hostess *Tante* Isabelle had been. The house would be a surprise for her. I wanted to start some work in the garden and I knew her advice and help would be invaluable.

Andrew insisted that I not accompany him to the airport.

"I want to be able to close my eyes and see you at the door, not in a lonely terminal. I will write to you occasionally but don't write to me, it's too dangerous. If you need me you only have to send a message. As I told you, it will be a long year, but I'll be back," he said with firm conviction.

He carried his bag and walked down to the cab. The driver took his bag and Andrew returned to where I was standing.

"I should have one kiss to last me a year," he said as he took me in his arms. He held me tightly against him for a few moments and then lowered his head and found my mouth.

It was lonely with Andrew gone but I threw myself into work. My house was looking fabulous. Spring was almost here. I'd wait for my aunt's visit to start the garden. Henrie and Adele were excellent servants and they saw to my every need.

I was having a hard time coming to terms with not having a job. I missed the excitement of my various assignments. I caught myself wishing I was working.

One night lying in bed unable to sleep, I got the idea to try my hand at writing. My life had taken some strange turns and might be of interest enough to make a successful book. It surprised me, the ease with which I fell into a routine of writing three to four hours a day. I must admit that some days were spent musing about my past, Enrique, and my future.

Aunt Betty arrived in Paris on the first official day of spring. I met her there and we purchased me a small car and packed it with all the things we found to buy for the house. We took the time to visit some museums and had some quiet dinners. She seemed pleased with me and what I had done with my life here. I was rested, had gained some weight and looked much better than when Andrew saw me last.

We stopped over in several small towns as we drove to Chamonix. She loved it. Most of her visits had been formal political ones to meet some ambassador or another, to ask a favor or to give one. She delighted in our informal trip where we stopped when we felt like it, ate when we were hungry, and acted like tourists, admiring all we saw on our adventure.

We talked constantly, each trying to catch up on what the other had been doing. I told her I had made a few friends and was anxious to have her meet them. She was looking forward to visiting with *Tante* Isabelle. It had been years since they had had the opportunity to really visit. The countryside was beautiful. Flowers were budding out and trees sprang new leaves. Green grass was stretching up to the warm sun. Little French cottages charmed us in every town we passed through.

At last we were home. Aunt Betty was properly impressed with my new home. She seemed extremely pleased that I had saved the garden for her advice I had always seen her as a pampered southern woman. How nice to be surprised by her willingness to help me do anything and everything that needed doing, even to ruining her fingernails in the dirt around my rose bushes.

I thought about how my image of her had changed on this visit. She had always been warm, helpful and loving, but I could not imagine her in any role except senator's widow. Now I saw her as the same wonderful person in and out of Washington. Maybe I was finally growing up. Maybe I qualified to be called a woman now, instead of a girl.

Andrew's letters were my connection with home. He didn't write often but, when he did, the letters were funny, informative, and described home as I remembered it. He kept me up to date with the office routine as if I would be coming back. It made me feel as if I was still a part of it all. He complained of his solitary lifestyle outside the office. He wrote that I had made him a monk, all other women paled in comparison to me. Boy did my ego need those words. He didn't realize how much.

He also wrote that he had requested a change of positions at the end of the year. He wasn't sure what new position, but was working several things and would let me know when it was worked out. I looked forward to those letters with increasing emotion. I thought of him often. I would catch myself window shopping and spot some object that I thought he might like. One day I had found an antique globe and had put it away for him for Christmas.

As the months passed, my memories of Enrique were delegated further and further back in my mind. It seemed to me that I had known him in another life. On occasion I would be reminded of him by a flower, a song, or an article, or something on Mexico, but I could smile now at those memories. No more tears, they had all been shed. My memories were sweet ones now and would remain part of me for the rest of my life. Life goes on and mine was getting there.

Aunt Betty ended up staying with me for most of the year. She was my rock. She watched out for my physical and mental health, encouraging me to the point of swelling my head over my writing. Together we had made a real home of 'Le Bijou'. She confided to me that it was the happiest time of her life, that she felt at last like a mother.

When I was well again, and the book was in the hands of a literary agent, she decided she needed to see how Washington had fared without her. I felt as if my heart would bleed to see her go but, as she knew, I had a lot to keep me occupied, and Andrew was due to arrive back in France in a month.

31

ANDREW IN FRANCE

My new position was in the American Embassy in France. I had played all those politicians who were so worried about my discretion. I felt like a little boy who had gotten away with the whole cookie jar. I knew if I played my cards right I could remain in this position until time for retirement.

I had decided against telling Natalie until we had talked of more serious things. Another thing I couldn't confess until we talked was that I had a wedding ring tucked away in one of my suitcases. It belonged first to my grandmother. After her, my mom had worn it until her death. My father had given it to me when mom died with the advice to find a better candidate than the first time. I was sure I had the right one, no doubt in my mind.

A month's vacation was coming to me and I had taken an additional two month leave of absence before starting at the embassy. It seemed a good amount of time to get reacquainted with Natalie and then to marry her before she got away again. I was feeling like a teenager about to ask a girl to dance for the first time.

That feeling stayed with me as I boarded the plane. All of my dreams and future plans were at the other end of the flight. I was nervous as hell. I had written Natalie the date of my flight and approximate time of arrival at her home. I didn't want to see her at the airport. Maybe I just wanted to keep my dreams safe for a while longer. I thought it was because I had this picture in my head of her standing in the doorway as the taxi drove away. I wanted it to be the same, to wipe away that year of lonely yearning for the only woman I wanted.

It didn't happen quite that way. I didn't bother with a train from the airport. I hired a cab to drive me right to her door. As the cab pulled into the long drive to her house I noticed the changes. There were more flowers, the trees were pruned and in top shape, the road had been repaired, and the house was as clean as if she had had it washed the day before. It was a beautiful sight to me. After the cab stopped, I alighted and took my bags. I gave him a hefty tip for delivering me so quickly.

As he drove away and I turned toward the house I spotted Henrie coming around the side of the building. He hurried up and shook my hand.

"You are expected and she is anxiously awaiting you," he told me. She had just gone for a short walk into the forest and wouldn't leave the main path, I was informed. He took the bags and I started into the trees to find her.

After walking about ten minutes I noticed a wide area in the trees. It was a lookout point. At first I didn't see her. She stood beside a tree and looked out at the panoramic view. She heard my footsteps and turned toward me. In her arms she held a baby. We walked toward each other and a million questions raced through my mind. As she got nearer most of them were answered.

I enclosed them both in my arms for a long moment and then said, "What's her name? Without waiting for an answer I said, "Give her to me. It's time she got to know her father."

We kissed with the baby between us and Natalie smiled. "Let's go home," she said.

32

AFTERMATH

It's strange how quiet and tranquil a house can be when the eager voices of children have matured and gone away. It never failed to get my attention.

Most of the snow covering the mountains surrounding Grand Junction has melted. Of course, it's time. Spring was late again, but June first is just around the corner. Today I spent planting those tiny plants, started in the hothouse, which always turned the back yard into a blaze of glory about the end of June.

Tempted by the deep shade of the giant aspen trees, I pulled off my gloves, dusted some of the dirt off my knees and sank down into one of the deep cushions that covered the white, wrought iron chairs. These chairs always remind me of Mexico. I can close my eyes and see the benches scattered around the one plaza existing for me only in my memories.

When we first moved to Grand Junction, Colorado, twenty years ago, María was ten, Pierre was eight, and Paul was four. Oh how they had complained about leaving our little chateau in France.

It was a hard decision. We could have enlarged the chateau; we were bursting at the seams. The final considerations were: is it safe, and do we want our children to be French or American?

We opted for the United States and never looked back. The big old house we bought has been remodeled twice and added onto once. We wanted it large enough to house our family and for grandchildren to come to visit later on. It had felt like a strange hotel at first, but over the years we have made it ours, and now it's home.

María and Pierre have each given us two grandchildren whom we love to distraction. María and her family left yesterday. That's probably why memories have been darting in and out of my head all day. Justin, her six-year-old son, smiles at me and the world can be his. His eyes are almost black and his hair is dark and curly. It isn't that the others are not just as dear. It's just different.

God had been good to me. My faithful husband has been beside me for thirty years. He is kind and thoughtful and a wonderful father. His children adore him.

Through all the thirty years he has courted me. During our ten years in France, he changed profession and now teaches French at the University of Colorado. He is much grayer and nearing a time when he must give it up to help me in the garden. His love affair with education, begun during our years in France, has been a consuming passion. If he couldn't help young people in one field, he would in another.

My books have satisfied my need for work of my own. I don't turn them out like an assembly line but the ones I have written have been well received by my loyal fans.

I have loved two men in my lifetime, both passionately. They were very different, but in some ways, oddly similar.

María has been told about her biological father. Andrew wanted to be the one to tell her. He was generous to a fault about Enrique's part in saving me and putting a lot of drug people out of business. I had tears in my eyes as he told her that Enrique had left him one of life's most precious gifts, a daughter.

María smiled that familiar consuming smile and jumped up to hug him. She has no doubt about the identity of her real father.

Nothing is hidden between Andrew and me. He has seen me at my worst and knows me at my best. He has driven away the nightmares and kept me safe. He even knows how precious Justin is to me and feels the same. A small part of Enrique lives on in one small boy, in whom we both delight.

THE AUTHOR

Born and raised in small-town Texas, Jan Dunlap has lived almost half her life outside the USA. Jan, who has a formal background in sociology, spent ten years in Puerto Rico, where she met Fidel Castro, and more than thirty years in Mexico, where she owned a restaurant-art gallery. Completely bilingual, she has always loved to write and has completed several novels and screenplays.

In *Dilemma*, the first of her works to be published, Dunlap weaves an exciting tale of romance, drugs and intrigue, loosely based on events and characters from her past.

Interested in the movie rights? Contact the publisher!

Look for these Mexico-related non-fiction books

Mexican Kaleidoscope: myths, mysteries and mystique (2016) - Tony Burton's wide-ranging collection of informative and often surprising vignettes gathered from Mexico's rich history and culture.

Lake Chapala Through the Ages, an Anthology of Travelers' Tales (2008) - Dozens of first-hand accounts of the Lake Chapala area from 1530 to 1910 provide a fascinating introudction to this popular region of Mexico.

Mexico by Motorcycle: An Adventure Story and Guide (2015) - Bill Kaliher's travels off the beaten track in 1971 and 1993, with travel tips and sound advice for the bike aficionado and Mexico fans.

Western Mexico: A Traveler's Treasury (4th edition, 2014) - Tony Burton's classic travel book that draws on personal experience and meticulous research to divulge the virtues and peculiarities of this amazingly varied area of Mexico.

Geo-Mexico, the Geography and Dynamics of Modern Mexico (2010) - Recommended for educators, students, and anyone with more than a passing interest in the culture, history, terrain, economy, politics, or development of the country.